Eric and the Woolly Jumpers

Huge thanks and much affection
to Phil and Tina Sharpe
without whom none of this
would have happened

D1513095

Malcolm Hulme

The Woolly Jumpers

Copyright Malcolm Hulme 2009

www.thewoollyjumpers.com

This First Edition published in 2010

The Woolly Jumpers
Mansfield Gardens
Hawick
Roxburghshire
TD9 8AN

ISBN 978-0-9566374-0-6

Get Off! We Got Things To Do & Pre Op Blues
Written by Mark Hulme

Cover Design by Jon Wainwright

Printed and Typeset by Dolman Scott
www.dolmanscott.com

PROLOGUE

Two billion years from now the world was a very different place. Mankind had destroyed his environment and consequently himself a long time ago. Over millions of years the Earth healed its terrible wounds. Continents moved and changed shape; species of animals came and went. There were ice ages followed by times of great heat. Finally, the earth settled down to a gentle rhythm, allowing an elite species to evolve. They were Emia Hopsons, not dissimilar to you and me.

Sophisticated civilisations grew quickly but sadly, as with us, military might reared its ugly head. One great problem they could never overcome was their fear of flying. Large navies were built and great sea battles took place. They fought each other for hundreds of years until finally agreeing that each continent should leave the others alone before they totally destroyed themselves. Over time an uneasy peace cemented itself and they all got on with their own lives. For the continents governed in a kind, democratic manner this worked well. Our story concerns one that was run in a very different way, a hideous dictatorship ruled with an iron fist by one man consumed by self-interest and greed. All lived in fear of him!

CHAPTER 1

ESCAPE

Sinisterly black, the car approached the Facility gates. On both sides of them a high metal fence stretched away into the distance. Slowly, the car slithered to a halt. One of the blacked out windows hissed as it was lowered. Dressed in black with a black helmet that covered its face a creature marched out of a hut by the gates, took a card from the unseen driver and pushed it into a slot in the wall. Clanging and whirring, the gates slowly opened, letting the car crawl through under a sign saying, 'Cloning Facility.' 'Top Secret - KEEP OUT!'

It was a long way from the gates to the Facility itself; for the last hour they had driven through an enormous forest, thick with trees. Now there were none, not even a flower: just a huge concrete desert that seemed to stretch forever. Patrolling this wasteland were guards dressed like the creature on the gate, but these were carrying weapons of some sort. If the car passed anywhere near they jumped to attention and saluted.

In the afternoon sunlight the vast, square, silver, eyeless Cloning Facility exuded malevolence. Almost noiseless humming sounds crept out of it, giving the impression it was desperately trying to be quiet so as not to give away any of its secrets. Faceless guards in their black helmets and uniforms were everywhere. Outsiders would have wondered whether they were there to stop things getting in or getting out. Part of the Facility wall slid to one side as they approached, allowing the car to enter then slammed shut with an ominous bang. Inside, the car slid to a halt. The driver, dressed like all the others, got out, walked stiffly to the back of the car and opened the door.

Generalissimo Walter Strumphh struggled out of the car with the help of the driver. What an extraordinary sight! Nearly as wide as he was tall, with short, thin arms and the skinniest of legs. He looked like a large, fat balloon with four knitting needles stuck in it. On top of the balloon was the biggest head you've ever seen, bald except for a tuft of hair on top with the smallest shifty eyes that were too close together, a truly enormous bulbous nose that overshadowed everything else, and a tiny mouth that had lived in the shade of the nose for so long it had never grown properly and was so sad it had never learnt to smile. Strumphh pushed his driver away, brushed down his dishevelled lilac suit, adjusted his bright yellow waistcoat that was so tight fitting the buttons pushed out dangerously, straightened his pink tie, most of which was hidden under rolls of fat as it disappeared into his shirt collar and placed on top of his enormous nose the tiniest pince nez eyeglasses. This made him look even more ridiculous but he felt it added to his already inflated sense of self importance.

Last out of the car was an equally bizarre spectacle: Strumphh's assistant, TD Beagle. Toady to his enemies and Toady to such friends as he had, which were precious few, if any. Toady was the skinniest person you've ever seen. His clothes hung off him like washing on a line. He was so tiny he looked like he'd fit into Strumphh's pocket. In lots of ways Strumphh did have him in his pocket so maybe it was appropriate. His face was thin and gaunt. Over sized rabbit teeth were crammed into a tiny mouth and eyes like organ stops stood out from his head. No matter what he did with his hair it always stood on end, giving the impression that he stuck his finger in a light socket every morning, thus adding to the general air of shock he always carried with him. Toady was always hungry, constantly dribbling whenever he was near food or someone mentioned the subject. It was thought he must have a serious dose of worms to eat so much and be so thin. He said it was his metabolism. Everyone really knew it was because he used up so much nervous energy being both terrified of, and servile to, Generalissimo Strumphh. Toady by name, Toady by nature!

Walter Strumphh looked proudly around, standing in the empty atrium of his pride and joy, The Cloning Facility. Nothing had stopped him achieving this, the jewel in his crown. Whilst he gloated a panel in the wall opened and in came a being in a white coat, a surgical mask that covered his entire face and a white hat. Saluting Strumphh, he ushered them into a lift and pushed the button marked Gallery Floor. Immediately the lift hurtled upwards.

'Tell me, have you solved the problem?' asked Strumphh.

'We think so,' said White Mask nervously. 'There are considerably less.'

'Considerably less! Considerably less! That's no good to me! I want none, not considerably less!' shrieked Strumphh.

'We are doing our best, Generalissimo, but it's a complicated process,' snivelled White Mask.

'Not as complicated as having potential revolutionaries running amok!' yelled Strumphh, his face getting redder by the minute, the veins on his nose fit to burst. 'They're out there now, plotting, scheming, trying to ruin my plans. Make sure you kill them all!'

'There are none in this batch. We've been very thorough,' he replied.

'There'd better not be,' said Strumphh threateningly.

When they reached the Gallery Floor the lift door slid back. Before them an enormous black mirror-glassed window looked down onto the ground floor of the Facility. Through the window they saw an endless stretch of white, slowly moving like waves on a gentle sea. It took a while to make out any distinct shapes in the huge mass but slowly it became clear that they were looking at an ocean of sheep, thousands of them, all perfectly white and utterly silent. Strumphh gloated at the sight laid out before him.

'I'm a genius, a total genius. Food, clothing, fuel, all we need from my one Facility, my dreams made real! My wealth will become inestimable. No one can stop me!'

Standing in front of the gallery window, arms raised aloft, he shouted, 'There has been no one like me before nor will there be again. I am Lord of the Geniuses!'

Through the blackened glass the sheep could neither see nor hear him. White Mask applauded politely. Strumphh turned from the window, arms still outstretched. Food consumed Beagle's mind and he failed to take in his master's speech until nudged violently in the ribs by White Mask. Realising his error, he started to applaud too.

Beagle started to dribble, muttering under his breath, 'Endless, glorious, beautiful food, meaty food.'

Saliva started to run in rivers down his suit before dripping onto the floor in front of him, forming a large pool.

Strumphh dropped his arms to his sides, looking at him in utter disgust. 'Much more of this,' he said, pointing at the sticky mess. 'And you'll be joining those sheep on their final journey!'

'I'm sorry master but the mention of food, it's too much,' snivelled Toady. 'Surely you could spare just one for me.'

'Never! We have targets, targets that must be met!' He looked menacingly at White Mask. 'Or heads will roll!'

'Yes master,' Toady said resignedly.

'Now on to the processing plant!' shouted Strumphh.

White Mask was shoved towards the lift. Strumphh turned on his heels to follow, slipping in Toady's dribble. Making frantic efforts to stay on his feet, he did a mad Irish jig with his two minions desperately trying to keep him upright. Faster his legs whirled until they were just a blur. His arms flailed like demented windmills. Button bullets shot off his waistcoat, ricocheting off the walls and Toady's head.

'Ow!' shrieked Toady. Another one hit him in the eye, making him let go of his master. 'Ow, Ouch, Ow!' he yelled as button after button hit him.

Strumphh's glasses sailed through the air, landing next to him, and whilst doing his crazy dance he trod on them, squashing them flat. Eventually his whirling extremities slowed down and with White Mask's help he managed to retain his balance but not his dignity. Facially, he was way past the colour of beetroot and sweat was pouring off him. The veins on his nose throbbed dangerously. Furious, he turned to Toady, smacking him on the top of his head. By doing so, Strumphh felt he had restored some of his lost dignity.

'Ow!' howled Toady, almost crying.

Strumphh tucked his shirt back in under the great rolls of fat that slopped over his belt like congealed custard and wobbled into the lift, shoving White Mask before him. Toady, still hopping and shrieking, was left alone as the lift doors slammed shut. Slowly he recovered his composure, hit the button for the lift and stood for a while watching the sea of sheep, trying not to dribble. Smug pleasure overcame him because he managed it for a while. He did it by thinking what he'd really like to do to Strumphh and what he'd like to do was horrible but it cheered him up no end. A demonic grin settled on his face. Momentarily, he had forgotten to be frightened. With a clunk the lift doors opened and Toady got in. The doors shut behind him. In the vastness of the white room below the sheep fidgeted restlessly.

If Strumphh and Company had bothered to look hard enough they would have seen something unusual amongst the white, shifting sea below them. One of them had a slightly different coloured woollen coat: fractionally dustier than the rest. They would have also seen that he was the only one wading his way slowly through the enormous ocean whilst the rest just trod water.

Under his breath, this sheep was whispering. 'Can you hear me? Can you hear me?'

The sheep nearby ignored him.

Continuing to wade through the morass he repeated it again and again. 'Can you hear me?'

Still he got no response. Again and again he tried.

He'd reached the far end of the enormous room and said it for the last time. To his delight, a sheep looked up at him, 'I can hear you. Who are you?'

This sheep was amazed he could understand this slightly odd looking stranger. His eyes were blue for a start. He'd never seen a sheep with blue eyes before and there were things about him that were just slightly different.

'Now listen to me,' said the stranger. 'Don't argue or talk back otherwise we're going be in big trouble.'

'Alright,' said the sheep.

'Keep your head down, stick to me like glue. When I say run,' ordered the stranger, 'I mean run!'

'Where are we going?' he asked.

'It doesn't matter, just do as I do, stop asking questions!' said the stranger curtly.

Whoever the stranger was, wherever they were going had to be better than being here where there was no night or day just the same flat white light, thought the sheep. We just stand here, waiting for food to be dropped from the ceiling before being swept away into another huge room. The floor's cleaned then we're pushed back into the first room like a wave crashing onto a beach and like the tide we wait for the whole process to be repeated again and again. It was so boring. We seem to be waiting for something, but what? The sheep was sure he didn't want to find out.

For a while the stranger stood still in the middle of the ebb and flow. Calming music started and a door opened at the far end of the huge room. Behind them a wall was slowly moving, gently nudging a wave of sheep towards the open door where they were swept through single file by the weight of the sheep sea behind them. Slowly, the stranger and the sheep meandered closer to the door until at last they reached it. They passed through into a long corridor where the soothing music was even louder. The corridor was just the width of a single sheep, very low, gun barrel straight, dimly lit and eerily green. At the end of the corridor was a bright light that got ever larger as they flowed towards it. Fear was everywhere, increasing as they drifted slowly down the narrow corridor. Every so often the thin river of sheep would come to a halt. In the distance the sheep could hear a whirring sound. A funny smell pervaded the atmosphere and the sheep around him were now very frightened. Some had started bleating. Impassively, the stranger stood there, waiting for the column to trickle forwards again.

Several minutes passed as they stopped and started until they were close to the end of the corridor. So bright was the light now it hurt the sheep's eyes and the whirring was very loud. By scrunching his eyes really hard he could just see, at the end of the corridor, in the room with the bright light, two things dressed in black carefully examining each sheep before they were allowed through a door on the other side. What they were looking for, he wondered? Ever closer to the light the column flowed. Stopping suddenly, the stranger pulled something from his thick woollen coat and started to prise a large metal plate from the wall. After a few seconds' effort the plate fell to the floor and the stranger stepped through the hole. The sheep hesitated for a second before following him, turning in the hope that others would follow; to his disappointment none did. They just kept meandering by, ever closer to the light.

They were now in an unlit corridor barely big enough for them to squeeze through. Eternity seemed to pass in the blackness. Blindly, he bumped into the back of the stranger. We must have reached the end, he thought. Metallic scraping sounds echoed back. Excitement had replaced fear. Wherever this was leading had become an adventure, a mystery! For the first time in his short life he felt really alive!

After much effort, with no little cursing, the stranger managed to prise open the metal plate he had been struggling with and it fell to the floor with a clang. The stranger jumped through the opening. Following him to the edge, the sheep looked down to see the stranger had landed in an enormous pile of rubbish. He hesitated for a second.

'Come on, jump!' whispered the stranger. 'We haven't much time.'

Obediently, he jumped into the horrible heap. The stench was terrible. It was difficult not to sink below the surface of the slippery sludge. However, with the help of the stranger he managed it. For a few seconds they trod water. Suddenly, the whole festering lot was tipped forward at an angle, sliding them into the back of a large lorry, the pair of them fighting to stay afloat. Slowly moving away, the lorry headed towards a building marked 'Incineration Block - Rubbish only.'

Only seconds passed before the stranger pulled the sheep to the edge, saying, 'When I jump, you jump!'

At almost the same instant the stranger threw himself off the lorry. Wild with excitement, desperate to get out of the rotting rubbish, the sheep followed him.

Concrete hurtled towards him. Landing with a thud he rolled over and over, finishing up in a knotted-limb heap. Unhurt and unknotted, he got to his feet to see the stranger running at enormous speed towards the fence that surrounded the concrete floored Facility. Outside, a verdant green forest replaced the man made desert. Quickly he sped after him. Shouts echoed around, alarms started to ring. Bangs rent the air and bits of the concrete desert flew dangerously past him. Glancing back, he saw a mass of things in black charging after them. More bangs echoed around. Some way in front the stranger had stopped and was holding a long pole. As he reached him, the stranger said, 'Get on my back! Hold tight!'

No second invitation was necessary. Holding the long pole out in front of him the stranger started to run at enormous speed towards the fence. Faster, faster he went, so fast it was difficult for the sheep to hang on but using all his strength he just managed it. As the fence sped ever nearer the sheep saw a sign saying: 'Electric Fence - Danger Of Death – Keep Away!' Suddenly, the stranger dug the long pole into the ground; it bent backwards then whipped forward, flinging them skywards. They soared towards the deadly fence but not high enough! Pulling back harder on the pole they sailed higher and higher, close to the very top but still not high enough! As the fence hurtled ever nearer the sheep closed his eyes, fearing the worst. With one last Herculean effort the stranger used all his strength to force them just that little bit higher and they cleared it by less than an inch. The stranger let go of the pole and it hit the fence, burning to a crisp, leaving just a pile of smouldering ash. On they careered, landing on top of each other. Hardly daring to open his eyes the sheep was amazed to still be alive.

Then an odd thing started to happen: before his very eyes the stranger's woollen coat started to get slowly darker and a blazing, Olympic-like fiery torch appeared down each side of him. The flames flickered as he moved. The sheep was mesmerised. Turning to see if he was all right, gesturing for him to follow, the stranger disappeared into the forest.

Behind them they heard the things in black running after them, shouting and cursing. More bangs assaulted him. The sheep had no time for fear. Unseen phantoms seemed to zip past him, breaking branches from trees. Strength coursed through him as he got further from that awful place. By now the stranger's coat was dark brown and the flaming torches burnt brightly on his sides.

CHAPTER 2

LOST

Desperately trying to keep up, the sheep followed down little paths, turning right here, left there. He obviously knows where he's going, he thought. Still they could hear the shouts and bangs from behind but not quite so loudly.

They entered a little clearing; to the sheep's horror one of the things in black stepped into their path, aiming something at them but before he could do anything the stranger leapt from an enormous distance, knocking him flying into the bushes. Another came running in as they rushed by, firing something at the sheep. There was a huge bang! Something hit him hard, knocking him over. It really hurt but seemed to have done no real damage. Blind panic overcame him. Instead of following the stranger who had turned to the right the sheep charged blindly on, faster still, desperate not to be captured and taken back to that awful place. Off the paths now, running, running faster than before; through whipping branches, bushes, brambles, thorns tearing at his coat, tripping, falling. Just get away, get away pulsed through his mind. Get away! Behind him the shouts and bangs slowly faded, allowing fear to loosen its grip until letting go completely as silence became the only sound.

Exhaustion swarmed over him. He had to stop. Lying down in some long grass behind a tree in a patch of sunlight, he was asleep in seconds.

Waking up hours later he opened his eyes and for the first time since escaping looked at the world around him without fear. Whilst running away he'd been blind to everything except escape; now he could see, and how wonderful it was! He sat beneath an old oak tree on the edge of a forest, spellbound. The tree was high up on the side of a valley. Fluffy white clouds scooted across the sky, sailing on a warm breeze. The grass beneath him was dew covered, drifting slowly down the valley to a tree-lined river nestling below that wound its way along the valley floor.

On the other side the valley climbed away, dotted with trees. Flowers of the brightest colours were everywhere. Silence gripped the landscape except for the wind whispering a welcome through the grass whilst gently tugging at his woollen coat. Taking in the newness of it all he turned his face to the warmth of the sun, wondering if everywhere outside his previous life was the same as this, this beautiful. He hoped so. Hunger gnawed at him so he nibbled at the dewy grass all around, feasting until deliciously full. A pang of fear returned as he wondered if any of the creatures in black were nearby. He sat very still, listening, looking around. Relief swept over him when nothing moved or broke the silence. Slowly, he walked down to the river through the tall grass that nearly covered him, brushing against his wool, tickling his face, stirring some distant memory deep within. Perhaps he'd been here before but couldn't remember. Halfway down, there were noises above him. Looking up in amazement he saw birds fly past, swooping, twittering. Perhaps they were saying hello; he stopped and waved to them. Seeming to ignore him, they carried on their merry way. The sights and sounds were all so new! Full of the joys of freedom he rolled playfully in the wet grass. This new life was full of such promise. Where might it lead? Getting up, he continued on his way. Upon reaching the river he drank from the cool, clear water.

As he drank, he heard a movement in the bushes on the other side. An enormous wolf emerged from the undergrowth. The wolf stopped, looking long and hard at him. Filled with a primeval terror the sheep froze. Knowing he couldn't outrun the wolf, he stood there trying to look friendly and unafraid. Staring back with cold, unblinking eyes for what seemed an eternity the wolf barked loudly before disappearing into the long grass.

Relief swept over him. He knew the wolf was just as dangerous as the things in black. Maybe wolves can't swim he thought, relieved the river had been between them. After a while he started to walk along the riverbank before deciding he had to get to the other side to continue his journey. If wolves couldn't swim perhaps I can, he thought. The water looked cold and when he jumped in it made his heart skip. Paddling furiously, he floundered about, desperately trying to keep his head above the water. All he managed for a while was to go round and round in circles. Soon getting the hang of it, he headed towards the river's middle, enjoying himself so much he stopped and lay floating on his back with the cool water lapping against his face. Feeling adventurous, he flipped himself over, took a deep breath and dived below the surface, chasing fish that seemed to let him get close before speeding away. A great game it was! He played on until he'd had enough then swam to the other side.

Climbing out of the river onto the muddy bank, he shook himself. Water and dirt from his wool cascaded everywhere, cleansing him of all that had gone before. Carefully looking around before moving on, he saw no one, the silence only broken by the river gurgling as it sped by. Relieved, he walked up the other side of the valley. It was much steeper and higher. Time passed as he climbed to the top but when he finally made it he saw, way below, a vast plain stretching away into the distance. Fields of flowers etched its surface. Forests dotted it like the dark squares on a chessboard. Rivers vanished and reappeared as they meandered through them. How huge it looked as it disappeared over the far horizon. There was something strange though, barely visible; far, far away were smoke smudges, lots of them. They circled his entire view like a flickering grey wall. For a second he wondered what they were but didn't dwell on it, there was so much more to see.

Horror-struck, he saw a long column of the creatures in black appear down below. They looked like a long black serpent as they slithered through the fields. Even from a distance they seemed agitated; occasionally one or two would break off the snake, run into some trees then rejoin amidst much waving of pointed things. Suddenly, it popped into the sheep's head that the pointed things were guns. Crouching even lower, fighting the fear that muscled its way in. What were they doing? Were they looking for him or the stranger?

Thinking it best to stay where he was for a while he watched the sun start to set. Mesmerised, he watched the plain and the forests turn yellow, orange and a rainbow of reds before darkness swallowed them.

Having eaten some more he settled down for the night. Thoughts drove sleep away. How did he know all he knew? No one had taught him anything. He could read the sign on the deadly fence at the Facility. He could talk, he knew birds were birds, wolves were wolves, guns were guns and lots of other things, but how? More stuff entered his mind with the passing of every hour. Why didn't the other sheep want to escape? Deep down he knew something terrible went on there. The smoke, what did it mean? Where was the stranger? Was he looking for him? A terrible thought struck home: had he been caught? No, they won't catch him, he's too big and fast, clever too. Why did his wool change colour and the blazing torches appear down his sides? What did it mean? What was the best plan? Did he have a plan? Should he make one? All these thoughts bounced about inside his head like mad tennis balls until sleep won the day.

Dawn woke him, heat slowly pushing aside the night's chill as the sun rose higher in the sky. Stretching, he shook the dew from his wool, wondering what today would bring. Being on your own for too long could become lonely. Now he could talk he wanted to make friends and have long chats.

It took a long time to get to the plain below. The landscape shimmered under the baking sun. Trees danced rhythmically in the heat haze, making him thirsty. Slowly walking to a river, he drank from the cold water that swept by. I wonder if it's just me, the birds, a wolf and the terrible things in black that occupy this vast land, he asked himself? Loneliness shrouded him like a dark, damp blanket. He yearned for companionship, to see the stranger. Swimming across the river towards the other bank the water washed away his sadness. The stranger must be looking for him: you wouldn't go to all that trouble and not.

On the fourth day, halfway across an open field near a forest, two wolves came tearing out of the trees towards him. Terrified, he ran like he'd never run before. Barking loudly, the wolves were in hot pursuit. Closer they came, fangs bared, lolling tongues, cold blue, bloodshot eyes, now snapping at his heels, their hot breath upon him. Faster, faster he ran, faster still, faster than ever before and further. Running for what seemed an eternity then too tired to go any further, he slumped down. Looking behind, the wolves were exhausted too and had given up their pursuit. They stood on their hind legs, howling furiously before walking away.

Slowly, he tried to get up but his legs wouldn't carry him. Exhausted, he crawled into a clump of long grass where sleep spirited him away to safety. Inky black darkness greeted him when he awoke with a start. Stars twinkled down as he stared up into the night sky. He ate some of the grass around him before deciding to walk to a nearby wood. It would be safer in there, easier to hide. How his legs ached! I must have run miles he thought, limping slowly into the safety of the trees, listening carefully as he went - but there was nothing but the familiar sounds.

Lying down in the hollowed out stump of an old tree, he felt secure and slept again. In the morning the blanket of loneliness had returned, heavier than ever. For a second it entered his mind that he'd stay here forever, feeling safe, even if he was on his own. Then a strange thought occurred to him: I might be a special sheep, like the stranger. I couldn't have out-run the wolves otherwise. Maybe I have a purpose but don't know what it is yet. Anyway there has to be more to my life than this. All thoughts of giving up disappeared, replaced by a steely determination to go on.

Two more days were spent roaming the woods and fields, seeing nothing. Just as his resolve was beginning to slip again he entered a clearing in a forest. At one end was a small waterfall, splashing out from the forest's mouth, tinkling down onto green stained mossy stones where it formed a pool before being gobbled up again by the thick green undergrowth. Around the pool were wet rocks leading down to the clear, inviting water. Carefully picking his way down the slippery steps he stopped at the pool's edge.

About to sit down, a shrill voice screamed. 'Watch out! You're going to squash me!'

Nearly jumping out of his woollen coat, he just stopped himself. Looking underneath him and all around, there was nothing to be seen.

'Can't see me, can you?' said the voice. 'Clever isn't it!'

Heart beating fast, for all sorts of reasons, the sheep replied, 'Yes, but what if I'd sat on you?'

'I'm fast too,' said the voice. 'I'd have got out of the way.'

Looking harder, there was still nothing.

'Still can't see me can you, you're looking right at me. I'll give you a clue.'

The sheep continued to stare at the same spot. Slowly, the pattern of the rocks changed slightly. First, there was the outline of a pair of enormous wings then a body and finally a head. Quick as a flash the shape flew off the rock and disappeared into the forest.

Fearing he'd lost his newfound friend, 'Where are you now?'

'In the trees having a rest, it's hard work staying that colour for so long. I'm having a good look at you.'

'I promise I won't hurt you, I haven't spoken to anyone for ages, please come out and have a chat.'

'Alright.'

In a few seconds the most beautiful butterfly appeared, circling gracefully around him. His wings were at least five inches across, the most magnificent blood red with grey edging to the front that slowly became redder as it descended the wings. Fluttering in front of the sheep the light shone through his wafer thin wings, making them glow. His torso was thin and grey, two large green eyes protruded from a small head and long antennae with small blue, bud-like ends sprouted from the top of it. Tiny hairs covered his entire face and body. Finally, the butterfly landed on a branch opposite the sheep.

'Can all butterflies talk?' asked the sheep.

'No, only me!'

'How come?'

'That's easy. One day, I flew over a big silver building. Feeling rather tired, I thought I'd land on the roof and catch up on my beauty sleep.

30

Creatures as lovely as I need lots of it you know. Anyway, I passed over a chimney that puffed out a little cloud of steam. Unable to avoid it, I went straight through. Well, I can tell you as soon it touched me I began to feel most strange! I landed with a bump and my head began to spin like a top. I don't remember whether I went to sleep or fainted. One thing I can say is, when I came round, how my poor body ached! I could barely move my beautiful wings - but strangest of all, the buds on my antennae had turned blue! Sometime later, my strength returned. As I took off from the building's edge I saw two creatures in black masks. I swooped down to have a closer look. They were jabbering at each other. Wonder of wonders! I could understand them! As you can imagine, after that dreadful experience my mood was rather black so I thought I'd give them a piece of my mind. I shouted a few choice insults at them; they stared in amazement before responding in kind! Having given as good as I'd got I flew off, and here I am, the only talking butterfly in the land.'

'What an amazing story,' replied the sheep. 'How clever you are, and if I may say, the most beautiful colour.'

'I can change colour too, it's called camouflage you know,' bragged the butterfly.

'Very impressive,' said the sheep.

'I'll show you something really impressive. Watch this.'

With that the butterfly landed on the end of his nose.

'Now keep very still,' ordered the butterfly.

So close was the butterfly he had to go cross eyed to focus on his new friend.

'What are you going to do?'

'Keep quiet! I'm concentrating!' came the shrill reply.

Obediently, he kept very still and silent. Spreading his wings, the butterfly began to huff and puff. His cheeks blew out as he strained and strained. His face turned redder and redder. Little beads of sweat appeared on his antenna buds. Slowly, very slowly his wings began to turn blue. Huffing, puffing, sweating all the more until his wings finally stopped changing colour. What a wonderful shade of blue, like the sky but somehow richer, perhaps the blue as dusk turns to night, thought the sheep.

'There you are, done it!' gasped the exhausted butterfly. 'I've matched the colour of your eyes. A tricky one that but I did it in the end.'

His head was beginning to ache with being cross eyed for so long.

'Would you mind getting off my nose now please,' he asked politely.

Obligingly, the butterfly took off, landing in a tree opposite, looking proud, beautiful and blue. So my eyes are blue, just like the stranger's, thought the sheep excitedly. They match the butterfly's buds too!

'That's a wonderful trick,' exclaimed the sheep, his mind elsewhere.

'A trick! A trick!' shrieked the butterfly. 'That's more than a trick, it's a life saver. A trick indeed! I've a good mind to leave you here on your own!'

'Oh don't do that! It is very clever, and as you say, much more than just a trick. I meant no offence,' he pleaded.

'Very well. I'll stay,' said the butterfly, haughtily.

They sat in silence; he could see the butterfly was sulking.

'What's your name?' he asked after a while.

'Cyril,' came the reply. 'And a noble name it is too.'

'Oh indeed it is,' exclaimed the sheep. 'The noblest of names!'

The butterfly's mood changed for the better, his vanity restored.

'Do you have a name?' asked Cyril.

'No, I'm afraid I don't, not yet anyway: and I'm lost.'

'A sheep with no name, lost as well. How interesting!' mused Cyril.

Stretching his wings, he yawned loudly before folding them neatly onto his back. 'I'm so, so utterly exhausted after all that exertion.'

Within seconds he was fast asleep, snoring loudly. The sheep wanted to talk some more. Perhaps Cyril could help him in his quest. Trying to wake him was pointless; even if he did he'd be so cross he'd probably fly away. Night was falling so he settled down to get some sleep. Try as he might, he couldn't. Finally, after looking at the sky for hours he began dozing uneasily. What strange dreams he had. Dreams of all the things that had happened to him: escape, the stranger, creatures in black, wolves, Cyril, all mixed together into an uneasy, boiling, bubbling soup. Slowly, the soup drained away down an enormous plughole, leaving just blackness. A bright light replaced the darkness. Shimmering and ghost-like, the sheep emerged. His woollen coat radiated all the colours of the rainbow and behind him was an endless stream of his fellow animals with bright markings all over them. They were singing of freedom and a land they could call their own. Waking with a jolt, he lay there, wondering what it all meant.

CHAPTER 3

A NEW FRIEND

Later he dreamt that the white light had returned and was coming towards him through the forest, talking to itself as it weaved through the trees, sometimes singing strange, incomprehensible songs. Cyril snored, the waterfall gurgled. Those sounds were real. Perhaps I'm not dreaming, he thought. If I open my eyes, I'll know. He'd been standing in the room between sleep and waking. The door to waking had opened, this dream had been real! An eerie light was edging ever closer to the clearing. At a distance it had no real shape - just an incandescent glow. Now it was getting closer he began to make out its features. It was a glowing pear shape. Contained within the pear was a face, a kind face, a shining face with two sad, large eyes, two ears, a small nose and a big smiley mouth with bright teeth. Either side of the pear, about halfway down were a small pair of arms that were waving about as the pear sang to itself. At the top of the pear where the stalk would be there was a curl of light, standing up like a quiff of hair. A silver glow lit up all around it and the whole thing was hovering in the air. Getting down as low as possible the sheep tried to be really small. He didn't feel scared, just apprehensive; it looked harmless enough, even jolly, whatever it was. The pear had reached the clearing, still singing away to itself when it suddenly went quiet, hanging, glowing motionless in the air, listening. Crouching lower amongst the rocks the sheep hardly dared to breathe. He didn't think the pear was dangerous but he'd already learnt that discretion was the better part of valour.

'Hello, anybody there?' asked the pear.

The sheep kept as quiet as a church mouse.

'Oh come along now, I know you're there, don't be shy. I don't bite you know!' said the pear, beaming from ear to ear, glowing ever brighter.

He doesn't look dangerous or sound it, thought the sheep. Bravery, plus not a little inquisitiveness got the better of him. Full of apprehension, he stood up. The pear's smile became even broader, if that was possible.

'Hello, hello indeed, what a joy!' he cried. 'And to whom do I have the pleasure of addressing?'

Nervous still, the sheep took a step backwards.

'Oh don't be frightened, there's nothing to be afraid of. Please don't run away like everyone else!' pleaded the pear. The smile had gone, replaced by a look of sadness. 'I mean no harm. I'm so lonely.'

The sheep looked sadly at the pear's sadness. Loneliness was something he also knew. No longer backing away, he tried to smile. Immediately the pear beamed back at him so broadly the sheep thought if his smile got any wider it would hurt.

'That's better,' said the pear, glowing brightly. 'Much better! Let me see now, you're a sheep, Ovis Aries if I'm not much mistaken.'

'I don't know about Ovis Aries but I'm definitely a sheep,' he replied, apprehension draining away.

'Oh yes, definitely Ovis Aries and a fine looking one if I may say. Ovis Aries, a name from long, long ago!' cried the pear enthusiastically.

'If I'm an Ovis Aries, what are you?' asked the sheep.

'A most interesting question! One that over the years I've pondered long and hard. I can't answer I'm afraid: you see, I've forgotten.'

'How can you forget who you are?' asked the sheep, perplexed by this strange stranger.

'Oh, when you're as old as me it's easily done,' said the pear. 'Most easily done indeed!'

'How old are you?' enquired the sheep.

'Let me see,' said the pear. 'I'll have a good think.'

Hovering there for a few seconds, he suddenly whizzed high into the air. Fiercely coloured numbers shot out of him in a huge fountain like a firework display. Ghostly glowing geometry gyrated grimly over the sheep, cascading down on him like flaming confetti, making him duck. Colourful conundrums careered carelessly causing crazy cosmic collisions. Fiery formulas fizzed forth fiercesome fractions that hung in the air before disappearing only to be replaced by longer, more complicated ones that blazed brightly. Shiny sums soared skywards showering sparks, slowly turning into acrid algebra. Looking on, the sheep was amazed and dumbfounded as the night sky shone with light from the mathematical pyrotechnics.

Eventually, the pear's gyrations slowed, finally stopping in a last huge shower of multicoloured calculations.

'Eureka! I have it!' cried the pear. 'Good gracious me, I'm four billion years old give or take the odd millennium. How extraordinary!'

'No one's that old, even I know that!' retorted the sheep.

'My dear Ovis Aries, that depends on where you're from!' said the pear. 'Why I know beings far, far older than I, yes indeed, far older.'

'How can that be?' asked the sheep.

'When you've travelled as far as me you see and learn the most wonderful things!' cried the pear.

'Where are you from?' asked the sheep.

Sighing sadly, the pear said, 'I don't know anymore, I'm lost,' pointing at the dark sky. 'I'm from up there somewhere, an awfully, awfully long, long way away.'

Looking at the stars twinkling brightly the sheep tried to grasp the vastness of it all.

Deciding to come back to earth, the sheep continued, 'I know where I came from, a terrible place. I escaped with the help of another sheep but now I'm lost too.' Then a thought occurred to him. 'Perhaps we can help each other.'

'My dear fellow, that would be absolutely marvellous! A friend at last! Hurrah!' cried the pear, glowing ever brighter.

'Why don't you have any friends? You seem so nice,' asked the sheep.

Looking sad again, the pear replied. 'My appearance frightens everybody. They run away before they get to know me. Perhaps they think I'm a ghost.'

Hardly had he finished speaking when a shrill shriek burst from the trees. 'Get it away! Oh please get it away! The fright will surely kill me if you don't.'

Cyril was flying wildly about, lit up in the darkness by the pear's glow.

'See what I mean,' said the pear sadly.

'It's alright, he won't hurt you,' said the sheep soothingly.

'Yes it will. Yes it will! Look at it! It's not natural! Oh please make it go away,' wailed Cyril. 'If you do, I'll be your friend forever!'

Landing on a large leaf, he slowly made himself disappear.

'My oh my, that is clever. Look at that! Well I mean you can't look at it can you, he's disappeared! Ha Ha!' laughed the pear, pleased at his little joke.

'Go away, please go away, I'll expire I tell you, I'm feeling so terribly faint!' moaned Cyril.

Becoming visible again, Cyril appeared to be losing his grip on the leaf. Running over, the sheep stood under him. Cyril, in a dead faint fell gently onto his back. After a while he came round, groaning quietly to himself before burrowing deep into the woollen coat.

'It's alright Cyril, there's nothing to be frightened of,' said the sheep. 'He won't hurt you.'

'I don't care anymore,' Cyril said weakly. 'I've had it, I'm finished. My nerves are far, far too delicate for this awful affair.'

'Don't be silly, you're far too clever a butterfly to let this get you down,' said the sheep, playing on Cyril's vanity.

Looking up from deep within the sheep's wool, Cyril's nerve slowly returned. If the sheep wasn't scared, why should he be? If there was anything to be frightened of the sheep would have certainly run away. How clever I am to work that one out, he thought.

'Of course, I knew from the very beginning there was nothing to be frightened of,' preened Cyril.

'We knew that all along. A splendid joke, well acted if I may say. Congratulations my dear fellow!' chortled the pear.

'I'm so pleased you liked my little charade,' boasted Cyril, his vanity returning faster than his nerve.

'This is one of the happiest days of my life. Lost for billions of years, friendless, now I've made two friends in one day! How utterly, utterly splendid!' cried the pear.

Flying around happily, he glowed brighter than ever.

'Names!' he boomed. 'I feel formal introductions are in order!' Turning to Cyril, who was perched on the sheep's back. 'Let's have a good look at you, my dear fellow.'

Cyril, vanity restored, obligingly swooped around, looking as beautiful as he possibly could before settling on a branch close to the pear, spreading his wings wide to show himself off in the best possible light.

'Cyril, how delighted I am to meet such a splendid, splendid butterfly as your good self,' he cried enthusiastically. 'Allow me to introduce myself.' He paused for a second. 'Oh silly, silly me, in all the excitement I forgot, I don't have a name, do I! I know, perhaps you good fellows would be so kind as to think of one for me.'

'Good idea,' Cyril said. 'But it won't be easy.'

'Pray why?' asked the pear.

'You're not an animal so we can't give you an animally name, can we?' Cyril explained.

'Give me a for instance,' asked the pear.

'Well, how about Arthur?' said Cyril.

'Oh dear, oh deary me! Arthur! That would never do! How about something more,' he paused, thinking. 'Other worldly.'

'Other worldly, what does that mean?' Cyril asked.

'From up there,' the pear explained, pointing at the stars.

'I've never been up there. I can fly high but not that high,' said Cyril.

'Oh what a splendiferous game this is! Now come on my dear fellows, get those thinking caps on!' said the pear, whirling about above them excitedly, glowing fit to explode.

Deep in thought, the sheep said nothing; he was looking hard at the pear.

'I've an idea,' he said. 'How about inventing a name. You're not from here so here names won't do.'

'It gets better and better!' the pear bellowed. 'My dear Ovis, how clever you are. Do you have anything in mind?'

The sheep hesitated for a moment.

'Come now my dear chap, don't be shy!' exhorted the pear.

'You might think it silly,' said the sheep.

'Never!' exclaimed the pear. 'Now come on, the suspense is becoming too much. I feel quite light headed but I would, wouldn't I, having a light head, ha, ha!'

He whirled about above them, laughing at his own little joke, finally calming down and hovering quietly in front of the sheep.

'Come on my four legged friend, out with it,' he said cajolingly.

'Well I was thinking,' he paused for a second, 'I was thinking, how about a name that describes you?'

'Do you have anything in mind?'

'Actually I do,' replied the sheep. 'You always glow a lovely Silveree colour. What's nice is, the happier you are, the more Silveree you get. So I thought Silveree would be a good name.'

'Magnificent!' he bellowed. 'This fellow is a genius, how simply remarkable! What think you, my dear Cyril?'

Cyril was hoping he'd come up with a name but he had to admit it was a very good one and definitely other worldly, whatever that meant.

'Very good, very good!' said the butterfly, being very gracious, despite his disappointment.

'Silveree it is!' beamed the pear.' Now it's your turn my woolly chum.'

Not wanting to be out done again, Cyril said,

'I'm too tired, can't it wait for another day. I must have my beauty sleep.'

'He's right,' said the sheep. 'I'm tired too, we've all had enough excitement for one night.'

Cyril folded his delicate wings. In an instant he was snoring louder than ever. Sleep wouldn't come to the sheep, no matter how hard he tried. Silveree hovered about, humming to himself, beaming widely. Happiness warmed the sheep with an inner glow. He'd met some friends at last and by thinking of a name had cheered someone else up. Where was Silveree from? How had he got here? He must have been so lonely for all that time. How important good friends are, he thought.

'Indeed they are, indeed they are,' exclaimed Silveree.

Surprised, the sheep said. 'Can you read my mind? I was just thinking that.'

'Goodness gracious me no! You were half asleep, muttering under your breath,' exclaimed Silveree. 'I have powers but not that one.'

Sitting up, wide awake now, the sheep asked, 'What powers?'

'Let me see now. Well, for a start I never need sleep, food or water,' explained Silveree.

'You mean you never get hungry? I have to eat all the time otherwise I get tired and cross.'

'That, my dear woolly friend is because you are a sheep. Whilst I may have forgotten who I am, I know what I'm not, and Ovis Aries I am most definitely not.'

'How did you get lost?'

'I wish I knew. I've spent millions of years trying to remember but I can't,' said Silveree unhappily, his glow becoming ever dimmer.

'Don't be sad, I'm sure we'll think of something,' said the sheep encouragingly. 'You've friends now. Come on! Cheer up! This is a new beginning!'

'By Jove you're right! Things are indeed on the up! Best look to the future!' Glowing ever brighter, Silveree's happy face returned. 'Now you must tell me your tale, not the one on the end of your body but the other one. Ha Ha!'

Silveree hovered madly around, laughing at another of his little jokes, making the sheep laugh with him.

'Well, as soon as I'd escaped from that terrible place the other sheep and I got separated. Here I am, lost. I'm certain he must be looking for me so I keep moving on, trying to find him.'

'What terrible place?' asked Silveree.

'It was a huge, silver building surrounded by concrete. I was one of thousands of sheep inside. I escaped with the stranger but the others wouldn't follow. I just know something terrible happens in there,' he said, trembling as all the events in that horrible place flooded back.

'A stranger eh,' mused Silveree. 'Methinks it took a special stranger to rescue a special sheep.'

'Me? Special?'

'The others didn't follow did they? What does that tell you?'

'Perhaps they didn't understand the stranger,' said the sheep.

'But you did, therefore you're special. You have blue eyes and your wool is definitely not white.'

'Yes it is.'

'Look at a reflection of yourself in the pool, I think you might be in for a surprise!'

Silveree led the way to the pool, hovering above it, shining as brightly as he could. Leaning over, the sheep looked at his reflection. Gasping, he stepped backwards in a state of shock. Dumbfounded, he slumped to the ground. Words refused to leave his mouth, no matter how hard he tried.

Stammering, he tried to regain some of his composure.

'Did I,' he stuttered. 'Did I really see what I thought I saw?'

'Yes, my special little Ovis Aries, you most certainly did!' smiled Silveree.

'What, how, when?' he asked, breathlessly.

'In the last ten minutes, I watched it happen. I didn't say anything because I couldn't believe it myself. A sheep with a coat of many colours. How beautiful you look, if I may be so bold as to say.'

Hardly daring to look again, he hesitated before peering at his reflection. Silveree was right! Rainbow colours burst forth from his coat, shining softly in the night air. There were blues, reds, greens, yellows and all the colours in between. Astonished, he sat down again.

'I dreamt I had a coat like this! What does it mean Silveree?'

'A dream eh? Interesting, most interesting! Who understands the workings of the mind so well as to answer that one? Not me, my rainbow chum. One thing I do know my dear boy, you're special just like your rescuer.'

'His coat changed colour too.'

'Well I never, well I never. Extraordinary, most extraordinary!'

Muttering to himself, Silveree hovered slowly round the clearing for a while deep in thought whilst the sheep sat below, bemused by all that had happened.

'Splendid, splendid,' he cried. 'I have it. We must find your rescuer at once.'

'That won't be easy, this is a big place.'

'Ah, but I can travel faster than you, my brightly coloured companion.'

'How fast?'

'I can travel at the speed of thought!' exclaimed Silveree. 'The greatest of my somewhat modest talents.'

'How do you do it?' asked the sheep, believing anything was possible after the events of the last few hours.

'It's easy. I just think hard about where I want to go and I'm there in a flash!'

'So why can't you think of home and off you go?'

'I don't want to go home now I've met you and Cyril. I feel an adventure coming on. Oh yes, an adventure!'

'But could you if you wanted to?'

'There's one problem with thought travel; you have to know where you're going. As you know, I've forgotten where home is.'

'I see,' said the sheep, not sure if he fully understood. 'How will you find the stranger if you don't know where you're going?'

'I'll just have a good look around. This place may be big to you but it's tiny for me. Remember, I've been all over up there,' he pointed skywards. 'Now that is big: jolly big indeed!'

Looking up, the sheep had to agree. Up there looked enormous. Thought travel must be an excellent way of getting about, he decided: you wouldn't get tired legs.

Cyril had slept through it all; he woke up and saw the sheep's magnificent new coat. Tell me I'm dreaming, it can't be true, he thought. No one is more beautiful than I.

Silveree saw him clinging onto his branch, 'What do think of that my dear Cyril, utterly, utterly gorgeous is it not? Such colours!'

'It's all right I suppose, if you like that sort of thing,' he said sniffily.

'Oh my dear, dear boy, nowhere near as radiant as your good self. No one could be as splendid as you, could they, my special Ovis friend?'

'Absolutely not! You can change into such wonderful colours too. I can't do that. At least, I don't think I can.'

'Well,' Cyril admitted grudgingly. 'It is a rather wonderful coat as you say, not quite as splendid as mine however.'

'No argument from me, my fair winged flyer!' chortled Silveree. 'Now let us all have some rest, what a night we've had. Simply, simply marvellous!'

Cyril was asleep before Silveree had finished speaking. Not needing a second invitation, the sheep followed suit. He dreamt of flying through space, his new coat shining brightly, leaving behind a rainbow shower of sparks. Silveree hovered overhead, glowing quietly, smiling from ear to ear.

CHAPTER 4

STRUMPHH'S RAGE

After news of the sheep's escape reached him, Generalissimo Strumphh's fury knew no bounds. Terrified, all the creatures in black had hidden as best they could. Toady was fearful, very fearful; partly because he was genuinely afraid of his master. Afraid too, because he could see the funny side of it and was worried about smirking at the wrong moment. Knowing what was coming, White Mask prepared to face the music. Generalissimo was in his enormous office staring moodily at his favourite painting of himself. Every inch of the walls was covered in them. All the portraits showed him leering down haughtily in differing, brightly coloured uniforms. He'd changed into his favourite, a powder blue ensemble covered with gold braid, and like all his clothes it fitted too tightly, giving the impression the whole lot could explode off him at the slightest provocation. Medals of all shapes and sizes festooned his chest. Jammed on his head at a rakish angle was a tall cylindrical hat of the same colour with gold bands all around it. At his side was a gold sword in a golden scabbard. White Mask was seated in a tiny chair, looking up at Generalissimo who was seated behind a raised desk on an enormous one.

Generalissimo glared down at him. 'There are none in this batch, we've been very thorough, that's what you said, am I right?' He spat the words like venom at the poor thing in front of him.

'We were thorough, Generalissimo; all our tests said there would be none!' White Mask said feebly.

'Your tests were wrong, weren't they, imbecile!' yelled Strumphh.

'Yes but -' started White Mask.

'-There are no yes buts!' screamed Generalissimo, striding from behind his desk. Pulling the sword from its scabbard he struck him across the back of the head with the flat side of it, knocking him off his chair.

'We've done our best; we've now perfected the formula. I guarantee there will be no more. I swear that's the last!' White Mask snivelled, picking himself off the floor.

Generalissimo stuck the point of his sword against his chest.

'Please, there's no need for violence, please Generalissimo!' pleaded White Mask.

'Perhaps, but it makes me feel better,' hissed Strumphh. 'You'd better be right. If there's one more of these, shall we say, irregularities,' he pushed his face close to the grovelling heap in front of him, breathing foul breath on him, 'You will be joining your four legged friends on their final journey! Do I make myself clear?'

'Very clear,' said White Mask, struggling to his feet.

'Now get out!'

Rushing for the door, he was gone in a second. Strumphh put his sword away and stood hands behind his back, continuing his wall-mounted self-admiration. Toady had his head down, biting his lip with rabbit teeth, desperately trying not to smirk.

Turning to Toady, 'Get me the head creature!' he roared.

Toady left the room, leaving Strumphh with his thoughts; they were troubled ones, tinged with fear. Sheep had escaped before but never had one been rescued by an accomplice, worst of all an accomplice from outside who'd breached all his elaborate security. This was a new development and a frightening one. It showed levels of intelligence that posed a real threat. They were obviously organised now and would move against him. Greatness was born out of action. Being a supreme leader he would act, and swiftly. Perhaps he was just being paranoid? After all they were just sheep, crawled into his mind. Someone as brilliant as him: paranoid? Impossible! This was a fight to the death. There would only be one winner! The genius Walter Strumphh! Filled with his own sense of self importance his mood improved.

Toady entered with the chief of the guards, dressed in black and helmeted like the rest, his body language reflecting his terror. Trembling, he stood before the great one, dropping onto one knee, masked face bowed.

'Get up wretch!' spat Strumphh viciously.

Hesitantly, the guard got to his feet, head down, shaking,

'You let them escape, imbecile!' hissed Strumphh, 'Find them or your kind will become extinct. That is not a threat, that is a certainty! Do you understand?'

The poor creature nodded his head.

'Get your pathetic species together and find them!' he snarled.

Bowing and scraping, the creature backed away to the door before fleeing through it.

Strumphh turned to Toady, 'Order the burning to be accelerated!'

'Yes master,' Toady replied, 'Immediately.'

Toady left the room, smiling to himself in spite of the threat. Never before had he seen his master this shaken. All because of some sheep, five at the most; they'd captured the other one. Grinning horribly, he hoped that Strumphh was having sleepless nights at the very least. Fear had gnawed at him for the last hour. Now thoughts of food flooded hungrily back. Dribble trickled down his suit.

CHAPTER 5

FOUND

Dawn broke as the sheep slowly awoke, blinking in the morning sunlight. Light was streaming through Cyril's wings as he yawned loudly. Of Silveree, nothing was to be seen. Where's he gone, wondered the sheep, getting to his feet and drinking from the pool.

'Good morning one and all.' Silveree said.

Looking around, neither the sheep nor Cyril could see where the voice was coming from.

'Where are you?' enquired the sheep.

'Behind you, my dear fellow.'

They both looked long and hard at where the voice was coming from but saw nothing.

'Stop mucking about!' shrilled Cyril.

'I'm not,' said Silveree. 'I'm right in front of you.'

'Are you invisible?' asked the sheep.

'I'm afraid so,' said Silveree.

'That's my job, not yours!' shrieked Cyril.

'It's not my fault old bean. You can't see my glow in sunlight!' Silveree replied.

'Perhaps if you stand in the shadows we might be able to see you?' asked the sheep.

'Splendid idea,' said Silveree.

Silveree retreated into the darkness of the forest and the two of them could just make out a faint glow amongst the trees.

'Oh this is too much!' wailed Cyril. 'First your beautiful coat, now this! I'm the only creature that can disappear!'

Furious, he turned his back on them, sulking like he'd never sulked before.

'Now, now my dear friend,' said Silveree soothingly. 'Your abilities are far greater than mine! I've no choice but you can become invisible whenever you want. Now that is clever!'

'I suppose you're right,' retorted Cyril, feeling slightly better, turning to face them again.

How difficult some creatures can be, thought the sheep, smiling inwardly. Hungry now, he started to nibble the foliage at the edge of the pool.

Whilst he was eating happily, Silveree zoomed invisibly above them, 'I'm off to see if I can find your rescuer. I'll be back soon. Don't go away!'

The two of them spent the day lying in the sunshine. Basking in the warmth of his newfound friendships and the security of the clearing the sheep felt as happy as he'd ever been. Questions still had to be answered but there was time for that. As the hours passed he wondered how Silveree was getting on. Unconcerned, Cyril fluttered about happily.

Slowly, the setting sun disappeared, lengthening the shadows in the clearing. In the distant half light he heard Silveree calling, 'It's me, I've brought some friends, please don't be alarmed, they won't hurt you.'

Silveree, glowing dimly in the twilight, entered the clearing, followed by two wolves. Terrified, the sheep was off in a flash, fearing the worst. How could Silveree betray him like this? No matter how fast he ran, Silveree was always in front of him.

'Do stop dear Ovis,' he pleaded. 'There's nothing to be afraid of. They were sent to find you. Look behind you, they're not chasing you. Please stop!'

Slowing slightly, the sheep looked behind him. Silveree was right, they weren't after him. Silveree, in the darkness of the forest, was now glowing brightly and looking at him with such a kindly face the sheep stopped.

'That's better,' beamed Silveree. 'Now come back, let me introduce you.'

Hesitation gripped him for a second. Silveree put a glowing arm around him. Together, they walked back to the clearing in the gathering darkness. There, on the other side of the pool, lit by Silveree's glow, were two enormous wolves with the same huge fangs and cold blue eyes he'd seen before. Cyril was at the top of a tree, trembling in silence. Fear enveloped the sheep. He started to back away. The wolves didn't move. Silveree hovered between them, smiling calmly

'Allow me to introduce Urho and Sisu,' said Silveree, waving his arms extravagantly at the wolves.

In a growly voice he said something to the wolves, who howled loudly into the night air.

'They can't speak our language,' said Silveree. 'But I have some understanding of theirs. They've just said hello.'

'Hello,' stammered the sheep, slowly regaining his confidence. 'What do they want?'

'They've come to take you to your rescuer and his friends. They wanted to see you first.

They trust no one,' Silveree replied. 'They've been following your scent for days.'

'I know, they nearly caught me once.'

'They've told me only one of your kind is faster than you, The Fiery Torched runner.'

'That's him, my rescuer!' cried the sheep.

'I thought so,' smiled Silveree. 'How splendid!'

The wolves walked round the edge of the pool and sat down next to the sheep. They didn't seem so fierce now. Close up, he could even see kindness in their cold blue eyes.

Desperate to see his rescuer the sheep suggested they leave immediately. Silveree growled something to the wolves who howled back in response.

'They say you must be careful,' he said. 'Hundreds of masked creatures are looking for you and Fiery Torch. You're lucky you haven't bumped into them already.'

'I saw some a few days ago,' said the sheep. 'But they were a long way off.'

'We saw some on the way here. You're in good hands with these two,' he said. 'They'll get you there safely.'

After further discussion they decided to wait until morning.

As the sun rose, they set off. Sisu led the way, sniffing the air as he went. Cyril had decided to come too but kept well behind in case there was any trouble. Of Silveree, there was no sign. They moved deep into the forest. Sisu would stop occasionally, listening, before moving on. Ears pricked, Urho suddenly stopped, dropping silently to the ground, hidden in the thick forest foliage. Sisu crawled ahead on his stomach before lying down, utterly still and silent. Far away, the sheep could hear voices, gruff ones, jabbering, cursing. They were getting closer. Now the voices were nearly on top of them. Heart pounding, forcing himself lower to the ground, the fear returned. Looking up a little he could see the masked creatures only feet away. Panic overtook him. He was about to run when Sisu leapt to his feet, charging madly at them, fangs bared, barking viciously, knocking some to the ground. Overcome with shock, they scattered momentarily before shooting at him. Sisu was through them now, running full tilt through the forest.

'After him lads!' one of them shouted, 'It's time we had some sport!'

Tearing through the forest after Sisu, firing their guns, they disappeared from sight. Urho calmly got to his feet and trotted off in the opposite direction with the sheep close behind. An hour passed before they stopped. Urho sat waiting anxiously for his friend. As dusk approached despair flooded through Urho; occasionally he would whimper. Unable to do nothing any longer the sheep put a comforting front leg on Urho's shoulder. Amazed, Urho turned to him, looking long and hard. The sheep was convinced he smiled. Within seconds he returned to his vigil. Tiredness crept upon them as dusk became night. Sadness overwhelmed Urho, who lay listless on the cold forest floor.

Suddenly, Urho's ears pricked. The sheep jumped to his feet. There was a whimper from within the forest. Urho was off like a shot, disappearing into the darkness. After a while he returned with a limping Sisu who staggered into the clearing before collapsing, blood trickling down his side. Urho licked his wound clean. Shivers racked his body, breath barely rattled out of him, dulling the light in his eyes. Death was slowly creeping up on him. Laying down next to him the sheep used his coat to warm him.

Death had crept closer still as the sun warmed his cold, lifeless body. Utter despair overwhelmed the sorry trio. I wonder where Silveree is, thought the sheep. Before he had finished thinking, he was there, glowing dimly in the early morning light.

Sadly, he looked down at Sisu. 'Oh dear, the poor fellow, this is too terrible.'

'Can you help?' asked the sheep.

He hesitated for a while. Desperation was etched on Urho's face. Still Silveree hesitated.

'Oh, if you can, please do something!' pleaded the sheep.

Silveree looked unhappily at his new friends. 'I'll try, but I can't promise.'

Still there was hesitation. Strange expressions appeared then disappeared from his normal kindly face. High into the air he zoomed, glowing brightly before dropping like a stone into Sisu's ear. Immediately, Sisu's body started to tremble and glow, his legs kicked out wildly. The three friends stepped backwards in amazement. Slowly, the trembling stopped and he glowed brighter still.

Recovering from the shock of what was happening, the sheep looked closely at Sisu.

'Look!' he cried. 'Look at the wound on his side, it's getting better!'

Amazed, they watched the wound on Sisu's side healing over in front of them! Glowing less now, light was returning to his eyes and he was breathing normally. Urho's joy was uncontained. He howled with happiness! Cyril fluttered about joyfully. Stunned, the sheep sat there smiling. Silveree reappeared from Sisu's ear. Instead of rising in the air, he lay on the floor, hardly glowing at all. Their joy turned to concern.

'Are you alright?' asked the sheep.

Silveree didn't reply. Distress radiated from him.

'Say something, Silveree!'

He looked up, pain etched on his face. Vainly, he tried to rise into the air.

After a while, he gasped. 'I'll be alright in a minute, just let me lie quietly.'

They stood back, watching him slowly recover. Gradually glowing ever brighter, he rose shakily into the air. When he was hovering normally he remained very quiet, appearing not to notice them. It's as if he's not here, thought the sheep as Silveree, eyes closed, mumbled under his breath in a strange language. This went on for a while before he came out of his trance. Smiling weakly down at them, he looked at Sisu, 'I did it, didn't I?'

'Yes you did!' chorused Cyril and the sheep.

Sisu got carefully to his feet and the two wolves howled their thanks.

'I'm very tired,' said Silveree. 'Go on without me, I'll find you later.'

For a second the sheep was going to argue but seeing the strange expression on Silveree's face, thought better of it. They waited for a while so Sisu could regain his strength before setting out on what the sheep hoped would be the final part of his journey.

CHAPTER 6

HOME

Hours trudged by as they walked across the vast plain with the wolves keeping a sharp lookout for any danger. Too exhausted to fly any further Cyril landed on the sheep's back, nestling deep into his wool. Finally, they entered a forest. Deep into the ever-thickening trees, bushes and brambles they scrambled until it was almost impossible to push through. Dusk was falling as they struggled on, deeper still. A high cliff appeared in front of them, rising like a wall out of the dense mass of trees. The wolves stopped, listening. How do we get over that, wondered the sheep? Sisu crept under some bushes at the base of the cliff and disappeared. Minutes passed before he returned - with the Fiery Torched stranger! The sheep smiled a welcome.

Fiery Torch looked at him, 'What happened to you?'

Deflated somewhat, the sheep replied. 'I'm sorry. I panicked and went in the wrong direction. I've been looking for you ever since.'

Fiery Torch looked sternly at him. 'Follow me.' He shoved his way easily through the undergrowth; the sheep followed. Alert to any danger, the wolves stayed outside.

They were in a long, dimly lit tunnel. Slowly it widened until they entered an enormous cavern. Amazed, the sheep looked around. So high was the ceiling he had to crane his neck to see it. Tables and chairs were spread around the floor.

'Wait here,' ordered Fiery Torch before disappearing down a tunnel at the back of the cave.

Cyril woke up and popped his head out of his woollen bed.

'Where are we?' he shrilled, looking around at the strange surroundings. 'I don't like it here.'

'It's alright,' said the sheep. 'We're safe now.'

'I hope so,' wailed Cyril, burrowing deep into his woollen sanctuary.

Alone now, the sheep had time to take in his surroundings. Carvings of strange machines, huge seated beasts, symbols, birds, snakes and animals littered the walls. Weird, wonderful writing was everywhere. A creature with lots of arms stared down at him in the ghostly half light. Propped up along the bottom were pictures and stone tablets. Cobweb-laden shelves of books and papers were everywhere. The flickering light gave it all an unreal feeling.

Paintings covered the Cathedral-like ceiling as it soared above him. They shone down on him as if they had a light of their own. He could make out figures in what was left of their brightly coloured robes and others that seemed to be flying. Near the centre were two hands, fingers outstretched, reaching out to each other. Looming over him, from the corner of the room was an enormous statue of an armless creature. What sort of animal is that, he wondered, awestruck by its sheer size. All this made his mind whirl.

Whilst trying to take it all in, he heard a voice,

'Hello, welcome to the treasure caves, your new home!' said the newcomer. 'Allow me to introduce myself. I'm Tien Sine, the founder of our little colony.'

'Hello, it's nice to be here at last,' looking at his new friend as he spoke.

Tien was small and thin. Above his lip was a large clump of thick grey hair that extended just past either side of his nose. On top of his head was a mass of long, unruly, patchy white hair that stood on end and blew all over the place. Written on each side of him in golden letters was:

$$E = mc^3$$

'Did you escape from that terrible place?' asked the sheep.

'You mean the cloning facility,' Tien replied. 'Yes, we all did. More of that later. You must meet the rest of our little group.'

Fiery Torch entered with two others.

'You've met our powerhouse, Nabi Stolu,' he continued. 'Without him you'd never have escaped.'

He thanked him again. Nabi nodded back.

'Nabi is a sheep of action and few words,' said Tien.

He's even bigger and more powerful than I remember, thought the sheep, admiring the blazing torches down his sides. They seemed brighter than ever.

The next sheep introduced himself, giving a jaunty salute, 'I'm Bardee Thron.'

'Hi Bardee,' replied the sheep, looking at the extraordinary animal in front of him. Circling Bardee's eyes were two large brown rings joined together by a thin strip that ran across his forehead. A dark brown band led from the

72

outside edges of the rings to behind his head, finishing behind his ears. Around his neck was a ragged yellow strip that flowed down one side of him almost as far as his hind legs. As he moved it looked like a scarf blowing in the wind.

The last sheep to step forward was an amazing sight: he had a brown face, long black braided hair that very nearly touched the ground and a mid brown body. Along his sides were coloured musical notes that danced as he walked.

'Hi brother, I'm Merly Boab.'

'Hi Merly.'

'He's our creative one,' said Tien. 'I'm the brains.'

'I'm just useless,' said Bardee sadly.

'Now, now, your time will come,' Tien replied affectionately.

Bardee and Merly stood looking interestedly at the sheep whilst Tien walked round him a couple of times before stopping and staring. Feeling uncomfortable, the sheep looked at the floor. What were they thinking, he wondered? They're all so different except for their blue eyes. Break the uneasy silence, he thought.

'Are there any more of you?'

Tien stopped his staring and looked sadly at the others who fidgeted uneasily. 'There was one more, but he was captured,' he replied, tears welling into his eyes

'It's too sad, brother' said Merly.

'I'll get him back one day if it's the last thing I do!' growled Nabi, a fearful look on his face.

'What happened?' asked the sheep.

'It was my fault,' said Nabi, ashamedly.

'Don't blame yourself,' soothed Tien. 'Let me explain.'

They all gathered round to listen.

'Arbe Sout was his name, much loved by us all. However, he had a brain defect in his left frontal lobe I believe. This manifested itself in a most extraordinary manner. If you asked him to turn left he would turn right. If you asked him to sit down he would stand up, if ... '

'Alright brother, we got the vibe.' interrupted Merly.

'Very well, I'll continue,' Tien tetchily replied. 'One day Arbe and Nabi were out looking for food when they were ambushed. Nabi made a simple error, an error any one of us could have made. He told Arbe to run. Of course, Arbe immediately stopped and sat down. By the time

Nabi realised his mistake, it was too late. Arbe was carried away by his captors.'

'He's not been seen since,' Bardee said, his voice filled with grief.

'All the animals in the forest have looked for him but no sign,' Tien replied.

'I **will** find him,' Nabi repeated with real menace.

'I blame myself,' said Tien. 'I should never have let him out of the cave in the first place.'

The sheep considered all this. 'I don't think it's anyone's fault.'

'Well said,' Tien replied, smiling at last. He looked at the sheep. 'Now our new friend, we get to you, the one we've been waiting for. The last of our kind.'

'Waiting for me, why?'

'Come with me, I'll show you.'

The group followed Tien to one of the cave's walls. Picking up a long stick, Tien pointed high up the wall to some strange writing and symbols.

'With the aid of the books and manuscripts I found here I have translated the writings on these walls.' Tien said importantly. He tapped the stick on the wall, next to some of the strange symbols, 'There are our names, you are the last one on the list. The writings below say expect a sheep of many colours to lead you back to happiness and prosperity.'

Pointing below the last line of writing to what looked like a small animal with a multicoloured coat, 'There you are in all your glory.'

Confusion overcame the sheep; he didn't know what to think. All the events in his short life were knotted in his head like unruly string. His dream, his coat, this place, what did it all mean?

Seeing the sheep's confusion, Tien said gently 'Let it all sink in while I tell you your name.'

Pulling down a large book from a shelf, he blew off the cobwebs and thumped it down on the table, creating a veritable dust storm, making them all cough. When it had cleared he started to thumb through the pages, sending up little plumes of dust, muttering, spluttering quietly to himself. Eventually, he found what he was looking for; he stared up at the symbols on the wall then back to the book.

'That's it! I was right!' he exclaimed. 'Your name is Eric!'

'Eric?' shouted Bardee Thron.

'Eric?' growled Nabi Stolu.

'Eric! No way he's called Eric. No brother of mine's called Eric!' cried Merly Boab.

'That's a stupid name! Why can't he have a proper one like ours?' demanded Bardee.

'Ridiculous!' Nabi said gruffly.

'Just Eric, nothing else?' asked Merly.

'No, nothing else, just Eric.'

'That's crazy brother, no one's called Eric, never mind just Eric!!'

'If you think you know better, you have a look!' Tien Sine said angrily, slamming the book shut, creating a veritable dust hurricane before stalking off in a cobweb coated sulk, coughing violently.

'OK, OK, you's the sheep,' said Merly. 'Eric it is. Though you gotta admit it's weird!'

'Weird it may be but that's what it says,' retorted Tien haughtily between coughs. 'The book is never wrong.'

The sheep had been thinking. He'd never had a name before. Any name was better than no name. Eric sounded good to him. 'I like Eric, nice and simple.'

'Good, that's settled,' Tien replied.

'I still think it's odd but if you like it, fair enough!' said Bardee.

'I'll go with the flow,' chimed Merly.

'Fine by me,' said Nabi.

Whilst all this had been going on Cyril had climbed unnoticed out of Eric's coat. Listening intently, he had forgotten to be frightened. Now, full of confidence he flew off Eric's back, circling happily above the group. 'I think Eric's a wonderful name, it so suits him!' he chirped.

Eric's four new friends looked up in amazement.

'Wow brothers, that is one crazy, beautiful flyer!' sang Merly.

'Purely a matter of physics,' Tien said, all knowingly. 'Let me explain. You see, it's simple really... .'

'Don't bother, it'll only give us brain fade,' interrupted Merly. 'We'll never get our heads round it anyway.'

'He can move though!' admired Nabi.

'Let me introduce Cyril, the most beautiful of all butterflies!' flattered Eric.

'So true, so true!' shrilled Cyril. Showing off, he flew upside down, looped the loop, barrel rolled and other breathtaking manoeuvres.

'Cool, brothers, he's really cool!' cried Merly.

Amazed by the grace of Cyril's flying Bardee looked on, enthralled. How he envied Cyril, defying gravity like that.

'As I've said, simply a matter of science, nothing more,' said Tien, pretending not to be impressed.

Exhausted, Cyril finally finished his flying display and landed on Eric's head upon which he received a spontaneous cheer.

'You're too kind! Too kind!' he shrilled, bowing and waving his antennae at his adoring audience. Bursting with pleasure, he milked the applause for all it was worth. 'Now I really must retire to my chamber, I am utterly exhausted, we butterflies so need our beauty sleep. The emotion is too much!'

Bowing gracefully a final time, he flounced away. Burrowing deep into Eric's wool, he was asleep in seconds. Tien suggested they show Eric round the rest of the caves. He was pointing various things out on the walls as they went when suddenly, singing could be heard. Accompanying the singing was a silver glow that slowly filtered down into the cave. Tien, Merly and Bardee started to back away down the tunnel at the back of the cave. Nabi snarled, standing his ground with Eric.

'There's nothing to be afraid of,' Eric said. 'It's Silveree.'

The three hesitated for a second then Silveree came into view. Terrified, they backed away again. Even Nabi took a backward step.

'Please don't be afraid, he won't hurt you,' implored Eric.

'Easier said than done brother,' said Merly.

'Hello, goodness me! What do we have here?' beamed Silveree.

The three sheep had moved so far down the tunnel all Eric could see was their heads. Nabi had backed away to the entrance, snarling ferociously. There must be something I can do, thought Eric. I know! He ran over and stood below Silveree who looked down on him kindly.

'See, he won't hurt me, or you. Come out, please!'

Nabi was the first to step forward, the others taking their lead from him. Stood huddled together, they looked nervously up at Silveree.

'My, my! What a magnificent band you are!' exclaimed Silveree, glowing brighter still.

'How extraordinary,' said Tien, his scientific brain beating back his nervousness. 'I must consult my reference books.'

He edged his way to a large pile of books, bought the top one to the table and opened it.

Concentration was etched on his face whilst flicking through the pages. Eventually he closed it, looking perplexed.

'Interesting, most interesting!' he looked at Silveree. 'You're not in there.'

'My dear fellow, should I be?' Silveree asked.

'Where are you from?' asked Tien.

'He doesn't know, do you Silveree?' said Eric. 'He's forgotten.'

'Silveree eh? Intriguing! You know each other well?' asked Tien.

'My dear Prof! We're old chums, aren't we Ovis?'

'He has a name now - Eric,' said Bardee.

'Eric. I say, how simply splendid!' bellowed Silveree.

'Ovis eh? You're a fellow scientist perhaps?' queried Tien.

'I've had the odd dabble with quantum physics and special relativity in my time.' chortled Silveree.

'Fascinating: come with me to my laboratory. We have much to discuss!' said Tien, ushering Silveree down the tunnel at the back of the cave.

'My pleasure, oh learned one!' smiled Silveree.

Happiness swept over Eric. He was delighted that Silveree seemed his old self again.

Turning to his new friends. 'Well, we've all had a bit of a shock this morning, one way or another!'

'One I could have done without!' Bardee said.

'He's one weird being,' Merly piped.

'Good hearted though,' Nabi growled.

'Praise indeed, brother! Praise indeed!' Merly said, amazed at Nabi saying anything let alone a compliment such as that.

Standing with his new friends, Eric began wondering what had happened to them. How did they get here?

'Tell me your stories,' he asked.

'We can't do that without Tien,' Merly replied. 'But we can tell you the problem.'

Sitting together round the table, Merly told all: 'Emia Hopsons, they're the ones that control our world, who we all escaped from. They're after us. They use creatures called Nokemys to do their mean stuff. They're burning all the forests. Soon we'll have nowhere to hide.'

'Nor will all the other animals,' Bardee said sadly.

'So that's what I saw!' exclaimed Eric, remembering the smoke smudges he'd seen. 'I imagine Nokemys are the creatures dressed in black?'

'That's right. Tien found them in one of his books. They're kindly looking when they're not wearing those horrible masks,' said Bardee.

'The worst thing is, they've speeded up the burning: we don't know what to do,' Merly said resignedly.

'We've been waiting for you: Tien says you'll know.' Bardee said.

'Me!' Eric exclaimed. 'Why me?'

'You'll think of something,' Nabi growled.

Eric's mind was a blur! All this suddenly thrust upon him!

'What about the animals?' he asked.

'They've settled their differences,' replied Bardee. 'That's why the wolves were looking for you. Everyone wants to help. We don't have much time.'

'Desperate times, brother, desperate times,' added Merly sadly.

'Why do the Nokemys obey the Hopsons?' Eric asked.

'Fear, my friend, fear. The Hopsons have a hold over them but we don't know what,' Merly responded.

'Why didn't the other sheep escape with us?'

'They don't have the power like us. They just go tamely to their ... ,' he paused. 'I can't say the word, it's too horrible!'

Nabi said nothing; sadness radiated from him.

'I understand,' Eric replied. He looked at his friends; he could feel their anger, frustration and tears. There must be something we can do, he thought. Perhaps Tien can help.

CHAPTER 7

TIEN'S LAB & TALES OF ESCAPE

They walked past cave after cave piled high with books. Weird, wonderful machines poked their heads out of rooms full to the brim. There were paintings piled everywhere and strange objects littered the floors. Tien's lab was in a smaller cave at the back. The whole place was filled with experiments of every kind. Test tubes, bottles, phials were everywhere. Glass tubes of all shapes and sizes soared out of bottles, high in the air like demented birds, swooping between one beaker and another, luminous liquids coursing through them. Bunsen burners heated colourful concoctions that bubbled and belched before streaming down tubes into chemical cluttered jars that fizzed forth smoke and vapour. Fluids flew from container to container sometimes changing colour. Grumbling gases were collected in bell jars of every size. In the corner a large copper boiler rumbled dangerously, steam singing from its leaking joints. Pipes ran from it, disappearing into the experimental chaos. In one corner, separate from the test tube forest, below a blackboard covered in complex formulas, was a battered, pockmarked table lying on its side. Chemical laden smoky steam filled the air; it was hot: very hot.

Silveree and Tien were huddled together, deep in discussion, studying a manuscript.

'Thought travel!' Tien suddenly exclaimed. 'Impossible!'

'For you perhaps, my boffin chum but not for out of body beings like myself,' Silveree replied.

'Can you demonstrate?' asked Tien.

'Yeh, Silver brother, show us your tricks!' goaded Merly.

'If I must,' smiled Silveree.

Closing his eyes, Silveree started to glow intensely then there was a flash of light as he disappeared. They stood there in amazement, waiting to see what would happen next. No sooner had they got over the shock of him going, he was back! Hovering in front of him was the most extraordinary creature imaginable. Small, four legged with feet like paddles; it was completely bald, with dark blue skin. Two large yellow eyes stuck out above a pointed purple nose. Beneath it was something that looked like a pink ice cream cone; squeaking noises were coming from it.

'This, my new friends, is a Ratnima from the planet Zorgron in the Andromeda galaxy,' explained Silveree.

'That's three million light years away!' cried a bewildered Tien.

'Close enough. Close enough indeed!' beamed Silveree.

Tien tried to reply, 'But, but, but ... .'

The Ratnima squeaked sadly.

'Now, I really must take him back, he doesn't like it here. It's not hot enough!' Silveree said.

'You could have fooled me, it's hot enough to fry!' said Bardee.

'Compared to where he comes from, this is positively freezing.'

Silveree repeated his disappearing act.

'Remarkable! Remarkable!' Tien muttered. 'So much to learn, so little time.'

Silveree was back before he'd finished thinking.

'That is one cool manoeuvre, Silver brother,' beamed Merly.

Bardee looked on enviously. Nabi grunted his approval. Eric just smiled.

'Maybe it's time for the newcomers' ritual?' suggested Bardee.

'Indeed it is.' replied Tien.

Enthusiastically, they all gathered around the table.

'Who'll start?' asked Bardee.

'Let me this time,' demanded Merly.

'No, the usual order: rituals never change!' replied Tien.

'Come on then!' Nabi responded gruffly.

Whatever the ritual was it seems really important to them, thought Eric. Cyril, now awake, sat on Eric's back, eager to see what happened next. Silveree hovered about in the background, looking at manuscripts and books as he went. Tien had told him all their names; he smiled when he saw the manuscripts and writing on the walls. Tien had got all the letters of their names right but in the wrong order. The only correct one was Eric. He decided to say nothing. After all, what's in a name?

Tien Sine struggled to get on the table but fell back and was helped on by the others. How old he looks, thought Eric sadly. Recovering his composure, Tien began.

'Many years ago, before the burnings started I found myself with all the other sheep in that terrible place. The Facility was much smaller. No walls surrounded it and the forest came right to the edge of the building. We were all kept in pens. There were very few Nokemys. No sheep had escaped before me so they didn't pay much attention to us, spending most of their time talking and laughing amongst themselves. Due to my enormous cerebral cortex I'd read the signs on those dreadful buildings. I won't use their names but we all know what they are.'

They all nodded sadly.

'Not liking it one bit, I vowed to escape. I tried speaking to the other sheep but to no avail. My reasoning abilities allowed me to formulate a plan. Slowly, I moved to the edge of the pen, getting as close to the forest as I dared. The day arrived for my batch to be.'

Faltering momentarily, he looked to the rest for help.

'It's alright brother, we know what you mean, just carry on,' Merly said reassuringly.

'Thank you,' said Tien. 'The fateful day arrived. More concerned with rounding us up and shoving us out of the pen than looking at what was going on behind them, the Nokemys gave me my chance. I simply walked into the forest and hid. No one saw me. Safe amongst the trees, I saw to my amazement a lone sheep sitting in the middle of the pen. A Nokemy went over, ordering him out. The sheep did the opposite. The more the Nokemy asked him to get out the further into the pen the sheep went. Due to my high levels of intelligence I realised that in order to get him to do what you wanted, you had to tell him the opposite! Taking my life in my hands, I shouted, 'Don't come here!' The sheep looked at me and came straight over! There was no time to feel pleased with myself as we'd been seen. Fortunately, in those days the Nokemys weren't armed! Telling the sheep that under no circumstances was he to follow me at great speed into the forest and if I stopped to hide, he mustn't, I set off as fast as I could. Looking behind me, there he was, hot on my heels! Youth was on my side. I could run fast, not as fast as dear Nabi but fast enough! The Nokemys gave chase for a while but soon gave up. We hid until dark. The next day I deduced that the search would start in earnest. That night we went on, trying to get as far away as possible. The Nokemys searched for us; occasionally we saw them. They didn't seem that serious about it. Only later did the Hopsons realise the significance of our little band. On we went, looking for a permanent hiding place. At last, we found this sanctuary and all its treasures. We've been here ever since. Science has been my life, leading me to understand the contents of these caves. Many experiments have been undertaken to improve our existence now and in the future. Over the years we have befriended the animals. Now we all work together for the common good. Sadly, Arbe our dear friend and my fellow inmate is no longer with us in person but is always in our hearts. There ends my tale.'

His audience applauded loudly. Silveree hovered above them, beaming down benevolently.

'Bravo,' he cried. 'Bravo!'

Tien smiled happily. 'Now it's your turn Bardee!'

Tien was helped off the table. Bardee Thron replaced him.

'When I came along security was much tighter,' he explained. 'Fences had been built and the Nokemys were armed. I knew I had to escape but during my awful time there I had never felt well. One day, I felt very faint and collapsed. Assuming I was dead, the Nokemys picked me up and threw me out onto the concrete in front of the building. Hours went by. I can only imagine they forgot about me. Day became night. Still no one came. Some strength was returning to my aching body. Using all my remaining energy, I crawled towards the perimeter fence. In those days it wasn't electric, just tall and menacing. Being small I managed to slowly crawl underneath into the forest beyond, whereupon I passed out again.

On waking, I was pleased to find that I hadn't been missed. Wracked with pain, starving and thirsty, I crawled deeper into the forest. The roots of a rotting tree became my sanctuary. How long I lay there I don't know. It could have been days or hours. All strength had left me. Eating and drinking were impossible. My mind took solace from the fact I had escaped, thus avoiding the terrible fate that had befallen the others. If this was the end, so be it. Giving up all hope, I closed my eyes for the last time. Strange dreams invaded my sleep. Wonderful craft carried me through time and space at incredible speeds into eternal blackness. Something was licking my face and nudging me. I was vaguely aware of being picked up and taken away. Darkness again enshrouded me. Time passed. Light started to infiltrate my brain; clarity slowly returned. I was here in this cave! How I got here I had no idea. Tien was giving me medicine and food. Over time my strength returned and the tale of my rescue by deer was told. Nokemys had been searching everywhere for me but thanks to their skill, to no avail. I thank them from the bottom of my heart. All I need now is to find a purpose for my being here. That is my tale.'

His audience rose as one, stamping their feet, clapping loudly. Silveree and Cyril whizzed madly round, cheering with them.

Bardee stepped down from the table. Nabi Stolu leapt upon it with an easy spring.

'My tale hasn't finished yet,' snarled Nabi. 'It finishes when I free Arbe! Nothing will stop me finding him as nothing stopped me escaping. That is all I have to say.'

They stood there, stunned and quiet. Eric broke the silence. 'Dear Nabi, brave words indeed. We will find him. You will be his rescuer. First we must make a plan.'

Nabi jumped athletically down from the table. Merly Boab casually replaced him.

'Do you want a tale or a song?' he cried.

'A song! A song!' came the unanimous reply.

'Which one?'

'Your first one!' replied Bardee.

'Ok brothers, are you ready?' he shouted.

'Yes!'

'Now give me that chorus loud and crisp!' Merly crooned.

He started tapping his feet as the rest clapped out a beat. Cyril and Silveree swooped around, moving to the rhythm. As Merly started to sing the musical notes down his sides bounced as he moved.

'Oh Alright
I'm escapin
I wanna scape it to you
We're scapin, scapin
And I hope you like scapin too

Ain't no walls, ain't no bars, and I'll get out anyhow
I am going to get to you
Cos in here there ain't no life, my soul does pay the price
Scapin til escape is through

We're scapin
To think that freedoms really gonna last

We're scapin
And I Hope this scape is be my last

No chain man stop me now, no prisoner get me
slow
In here never will grow old
Freedom must us unite. Then we all can see the
light
They'll never get my spirit sold.

Free's about my soul from that I cannot hide
To keep us satisfied
My life that now exist is the life I can't resist
So scape by my side.

Yeah. We're - we're scapin
We're scapin
See I wanna scape it to you
We're scapin
I've scaped. I hope you're scapin too.

Merly edged the song into silence. The entire
room burst into rapturous applause. Silveree
glowed fit to burst. Cyril barrel rolled around
to add to the entertainment and general jollity.
Merly bowed, raising his arms aloft, taking the
applause.

'More! More!' cried his adoring fans.

'OK brothers, give me the chorus one more time.'

Merly, the rest, Silveree and Cyril included, belted out the chorus again.

We're Scapin Scapin, Scapin. Scapin, yeah-eah-eah!
I wanna scape it wid you.
We're scapin, we're scapin; we're scapin. We're scapin,
We're scapin, we're scapin; we're scapin. We're scapin,
Hope you like scapin too.'

Merly leapt from the table, just before the end, landing amongst his friends. Laughter abounded! Calming down after a while, Tien addressed them all.

'There is one more story to tell. This one has only just begun,' he turned to Eric. 'You must lead us to the end of it!'

Responsibility weighed heavy on Eric's young shoulders. Tien noticed this and suggested an early night. They could talk more in the morning. Loud snores soon became the only noise echoing around the cave. Silveree smiled thoughtfully to himself as he looked kindly down upon Eric. He felt sure his new friend would rise to the challenge.

CHAPTER 8

A PLAN IS BORN

Waking early, Eric wandered out of the cave to see Sisu and Urho. Alert and proud they turned to him, growling a soft greeting. Smiling back, Eric sat down with them. Fresh air might clear my mind, he thought. A plan, I must have a plan. Ideas whizzed about in his head before fleeing out, rendered useless by new ones. There must be something! Then a lightning bolt of an idea struck him. Clarity filled his brain: it was so simple but would it work? Could they pull it off? Was it even possible? Desperate to tell Tien, he woke him up.

'I've had an idea,' cried Eric.

'Marvellous, I'll wake the others!'

'Can't I tell you first?'

'No, no. All for one and one for all!'

'Wake up, wake up, Eric's had an idea!' cried Tien.

Soon they were all awake and seated round the table.

'Come on brother, spin us the gig!' Merly crooned.

Eric hesitated, beginning to doubt himself.

'Go on dear Eric, you might just have it, you never know,' encouraged Silveree.

Cyril fluttered in agreement.

'At least you've had an idea, which is more than we've managed!' added Bardee.

'Out with it!' Nabi gruffed.

'Alright then,' he started uncertainly. 'What would happen if all of the sheep in the Facility were like us?'

There was a stunned silence. Tien paced about whilst the others took in the significance of it all.

Tien stopped his pacing. 'He's right! Just imagine! Tens of thousands of us, all capable of free thought: they'd be powerless to stop us!'

'What about the Nokemys?' queried Bardee.

'There'd be too many of us. They might even join us. They live in fear. Maybe we can convince them ours is a better way,' Eric replied.

'Leave the Nokemys to me,' snarled Nabi dangerously.

'No violence,' said Eric sternly, growing into his new role. 'We must not come down to their level.'

'But - ' started Nabi.

'Violence will not avenge Arbe,' Eric interrupted. 'If we are to convince the Nokemys it must be with words and deeds.'

'Nobly said, nobly said indeed!' exclaimed Silveree.

'He's right, dear Nabi,' soothed Tien. 'Who knows, we might even find Arbe alive and well.'

'I hope you're right,' growled Nabi.

'It's a great idea,' said Bardee. 'But how do we do it?'

'We'll never get in there. Even if we did, how do we change our brothers into sheep like us?' asked Merly.

'I have the formula. I've been working on it for years. All we need to do is replace their genetic soup with ours,' explained Tien.

'Oh that's alright then, we just walk in and ask them if they mind using our soup instead of theirs!' retorted Nabi.

'I know you're angry, Nabi. We must stick together!' said Eric.

'How do you know it works?' asked Bardee.

'I don't,' replied Tien. 'All my calculations say it will.'

'It's the only chance we've got, so we have to trust it,' replied Eric.

'There are guards everywhere! If we got in, where do we go?' enquired Bardee.

'That's where Silveree comes in,' explained Eric.

'Me?' said a shocked Silveree. 'Oh dear, dear, not again, no, no!'

'But we need your help. You can be invisible,' said Eric.

'I can't! I just can't!' Silveree whispered, glowing ever dimmer.

'Why not, Silver brother?' asked Merly.

Silveree was so dim now they could hardly see him. Strange expressions flitted across his face and the mumbling had started again. Eric could see his distress.

'Dear Silveree, what's wrong? Tell us. We'll understand - won't we?' he said, looking at the others.

They all nodded in agreement.

'Oh dear, oh dear,' Silveree said sadly. 'I'd love to help, I truly would, but you see it'll be the death of me.'

Eric thought back to Silveree healing the wolf and the effect it had on him.

'You're not allowed to interfere, are you?' he asked. 'That's why you were so ill after healing Sisu.'

'My dear Eric, you are the clever one!' said Silveree weakly. 'I've been warned; if I do it again I shall lose all my powers and be stuck here for eternity.'

'No more thought travel?' asked Tien.

'No more anything,' Silveree echoed miserably.

'That's a bad vibe, we can't ask him to sacrifice his box of tricks,' Merly added.

'No we can't,' Eric replied. 'I'm going to have to think of something else.'

The group watched Eric pace about, deep in thought. After a while he stopped and looked at Cyril. Noticing this, the others followed suit. Cyril noticed it too.

'What are you all looking at me for?' he shrieked.

'You could do it Cyril!' cried Eric.

'Do what?'

'Get into the Facility and have a look around.'

'That could be dangerous. No, no, impossible!' he screamed hysterically.

'They're not looking for butterflies, just sheep,' added Tien.

'You could use all your amazing talents. They'd never see you, you'd be a hero!' said Bardee.

'Be cool, flyboy, help save us all,' added Merly.

'This is really important,' Tien added. 'Otherwise none of us will have a world to live in.'

Being the centre of attention was good; being a hero even better; saving the world was irresistible.

'Alright, I'll do it,' he shrilled.

'Well done!' they chorused.

Basking in the attention, Cyril listened to Eric's plan. Sunrise would be a good time to leave, he thought.

CHAPTER 9

CYRIL'S ADVENTURE

Light slowly peered over the horizon as Cyril woke up. His bravery waned as the sun grew stronger. Butterflies aren't designed for this sort of affair, he thought. Danger loomed and he was frightened. There was no going back: once a hero always a hero. Think of the adulation when I return. What if I don't come back? No, I'm far too clever for that. Buoyed by this, he set off.

Flying over the plain, he headed for the Facility. Hundreds of Nokemys appeared and disappeared way below him. They mean business, he thought as he passed unseen, high above them. Eventually, shimmering in the distance, he saw the Facility. From high above he surveyed the scene. Guards were everywhere. Not a doorway or road was left unattended. Flying lower now, he had a closer look. Courage flowed through him and he flew amongst the Nokemys. None bothered with him. One took an idle swipe at him but he was way too fast, avoiding it easily. Careful, I must be careful, he thought. Flying over the building, he looked for a place to land. Enormous, flat and unguarded, the roof was an inviting airstrip. Delicately landing next to a large grill set into the roof, he looked around. There was no one.

Fear coursed through his veins. Outside, he had the freedom to fly. Now he had to go inside where he could be seen and swatted more easily. Invisibility was his only form of defence but it took time. Would he have the time? Heroics didn't appeal anymore. Home was all he wanted, someone else could save the world. All thoughts of going any further had vanished when he heard a voice.

'Cyril, it's alright, there's no need to be afraid.'

'Silveree, is that you?' asked Cyril.

'Yes.'

'I thought you said you couldn't help!'

'I can't, but I can come with you.'

Cyril began to feel better now he had a friend with him.

'Come on, in we go,' encouraged the voice.

Cyril gently squeezed between the bars of the grill. A straight shaft extended downwards. Cyril plucked up his courage and flew slowly down towards the bottom, where he landed on another grill. Underneath him was a brightly lit corridor. Voices could be heard, echoing up the shaft. Terrified, Cyril listened.

'The next batch is nearly ready,' said White Mask. 'I'm going to check on the mix for the last time. If we get this wrong, we're done for.'

White Mask, accompanied by a Nokemy, stood outside the door putting numbers into a keypad.

'This new system should stop anybody getting in: even the floor's alarmed,' said White Mask.

Cyril heard a door below him open and close.

'Go on,' said the voice.

Summoning all his courage, Cyril slipped through the grill and crept down the wall. Opposite him was the door.

'Now become invisible,' whispered the voice. 'Wait until the door opens then fly through.'

Desperately Cyril speeded up his invisibility process, his little butterfly heart pounding in his chest. Sweat trickled off him down the walls. Minutes passed. Staying invisible was getting harder and harder. He was about to give up when at last the door opened and White Mask and his companion walked out.

'Through the door!' the voice said.

Heart in mouth, Cyril flew quickly across the corridor, getting in the room just before the door was slammed shut on him. Collapsing on a table, he lay there, panting for breath. I can't go on, he thought. The voice said, yes you can, you must! Don't touch the floor! Look around you, quickly! A large vat stood in the middle of a pristine, white walled room. Metal rods stirred its contents. Looking up, he saw a grate in the ceiling, directly above a jar labelled Genetic Mix. Blue fluid was flowing gently from the vat into the genetic mix jar before being pumped slowly through a single tube that disappeared through a hole in the wall. That must be it, he thought! Now get out of here. Hiding behind the door, he waited.

Hours seemed to pass. Still no one entered. I'm so tired, he thought.

'Stay awake,' said the voice. 'You must stay awake!'

Cyril tried as hard as he could but eventually his eyes closed and he started to snore. How long he'd been asleep he didn't know but he was jolted awake by the door banging against the wall, dangerously close to where he'd landed. Quickly, he shot out of the room into the corridor. Round a corner he flew, straight into a group of Nokemys. They were as surprised as he was!

'Oh no! I forgot I'm not invisible anymore!' he moaned to himself.

The Nokemys swatted at him as he zoomed by, taking evasive action all the while. Panic stricken, Cyril hurtled on, faster and faster. More Nokemys appeared, flailing at him as he desperately manoeuvred past them. Finally he saw a metal grill above him and swept through it. Below him, White Mask and the rest laughed it off. After all, what harm could a butterfly do? He flew slowly along the thin corridor, desperately trying to find a way out. At last, another grating appeared above him and he sidled through it. Feeling cool, fresh air against his face, he sped away from that dreadful place as fast as he could until he could fly no more. Utterly exhausted, Cyril slowly glided down into the top of a tree and slept he'd never slept before.

When he awoke, his first impression was that it had all been a dream and a bad one at that. But no, he'd actually done it! Wait until I tell them about my heroic deeds, he thought. He'd have to thank Silveree. Invigorated, he headed straight back to the cave.

They were all there waiting for him. Shouts of 'Well done!' greeted him as he touched down. Danger lurked at every turn, he told them. Details were given of the genetic mix room, the alarm and all the other things he could think of. They listened keenly to every word. When he'd finished, he turned to Silveree.

'Lastly, even though my courage was unsurpassable, I couldn't have done it without your help.'

'My help? Why, my dear silken winged hero, I've been here all the time!' exclaimed Silveree.

'But, you were there with me: I heard you!' Cyril replied.

'Silveree's right, he never left here,' said Eric.

'But, but ... !'

'No buts, my dear Cyril. You're the hero and no mistake!' interjected Silveree.

Confused, Cyril thought for a second. Perhaps he'd imagined it all. He had no time to think further when Tien said, 'Cyril, on behalf of all free sheep we would like to present you with our highest award, the Circle of the Golden Ram.'

Eric walked over to Cyril and placed around his neck the tiniest of gold medals. Eric bowed and stepped back. Cyril did the same. Everyone rushed forward to congratulate him. For the first time in his life, Cyril felt quite humble.

When all the excitement had died down, Cyril settled comfortably on a pile of books. Still unsure of what really happened, he tried to work it out - with no success. He looked at his tiny medal. Written large upon it were the words, 'For Valour.' Hopefully, I never have to be a hero again, he thought, and maybe I have helped save the world! Smiling contentedly, he fell asleep.

CHAPTER 10

TIEN'S AMAZING MACHINE

Days passed in a frenzy of planning. The wolves had gone to warn the animals to be prepared for any eventuality. Tien was preparing **his** genetic mix under Silveree's watchful gaze. Nabi was training hard. Bardee lolled about, feeling useless, getting in everyone's way. Merly helped where he could, singing songs to keep them cheerful. Cyril basked in the glow of his adventure. Eric racked his brains. There was one problem he couldn't solve, not yet anyway. They had to get on the roof - but how?

Eric let Tien in on his concerns, 'If only we could fly!'

'Perhaps we can,' he replied. 'Come with me.'

Hidden at the back of Tien's lab was a secret door. Tien led Eric through into a truly enormous cavern. What he saw took Eric's breath away! Sitting menacingly in the middle was an enormous winged machine.

Eric gasped, 'What is it?'

'A Nepo Leara,' Tien explained. 'I found it here, buried in the sand. I've been trying to make it work for years!'

Eric walked round it, trying to take it in. The vast silver machine had three wings at the back, one of which stuck straight up. In the middle were two enormous wings, protruding sideways. Mounted on the under side of each of them were huge, strange machines that looked like lying down bell jars except they were made of a metallic substance. Coils of wire poured out of them like demented snakes. Under each wing was also a gas cylinder. Cables rushed everywhere, attaching themselves to flaps on the various wings. At the front, a bath shaped wooden frame was bolted to the whole thing. Enclosed in the bath were four seats. What Eric assumed were controls for the monster sat snugly at the front of the contraption. This was also home to a huge nest of cables and wires. The monstrous machine was kept from collapsing to the ground by three large wheels, one under each massive wing and one at the back.

'What do you think?' Tien asked proudly.

'Can this machine really fly?'

'Theoretically. All the information is on the walls and in the books in the treasure room.'

Eric, still amazed by the Nepo, turned to Tien and asked. 'What problems do you have?'

'I'm still working on various things. Harder still, we need someone to fly it!'

'I wouldn't have a clue!' said Eric. 'We must show it to the others.'

The others were called in.

'You cannot be serious!' Nabi exclaimed.

'I'm no flyboy,' said Merly.

'That won't fly, you have to have wings like mine,' preened Cyril.

Silveree circled it a few times before turning to Tien. 'How, simply, simply splendid!'

'Where's Bardee,' asked Eric.

'Moping,' explained Nabi. 'He feels more useless than ever!'

'I'll go get him,' said Merly.

Bardee walked sadly into the cavern. On seeing the strange machine his face lit up with joy. Fascinated, he walked round the monster, pulling on various cables. Crawling under the wings he inspected the wheels and anything else he could see. He looked into the bell jars, grunting his approval. Leaning a ladder against the front, he climbed into the wooden bath.

Moving quickly, he clambered into the front seat and inspected the controls. Levers and knobs fell under his spell. Delight consumed him as he watched the flaps and bell jars obey his commands. His friends watched with blank amazement. Bardee smiled inwardly; this was something he just knew. Perhaps he would be able to fly after all!

Climbing jauntily out, he dropped casually to the ground.

'She'll fly,' he said.

Tien stood there, open mouthed. Merly went over to Bardee and gave him a high five.

'What do we need to get it in the air?' asked Eric.

'Fuel. I'm nearly there,' said Tien.

'What's it made of?' Eric enquired.

Tien looked embarrassed, 'The animals give it to me.'

'Give you what brother?' asked Merly.

'Well, you know, they come to my fuel store and leave something,' he said red faced.

'What?' demanded Nabi.

'Hang loose brothers, I got the deal. They take a dump!' shouted Merly gleefully.

'Well, yes, if you must put it like that,' Tien replied sheepishly.

'A machine that flies on animal crap! That's too much, brother!' Merly replied, laughing hysterically.

Merly's mirth was so contagious soon they were all rolling about laughing, except of course Tien.

'I'm glad you all find it so amusing,' Tien shouted sulkily.

'It does have its funny side!' said Eric, wiping tears from his eyes.

Eventually the laughter died down.

'What do you do with the er, you know what?' asked Eric.

'I turn it into gas,' Tien replied.

'Listen brother, you don't need no animal crap to have some gas!' Merly sang mischievously. 'I can give you some now!'

At that he broke wind long and loud!

'There's more where that came from too!'

A gale of laughter tore through them all again. When it had finally blown itself out, Eric said, 'Well I think we should applaud Tien for all his efforts!'

'I couldn't agree more, my dear Eric,' said Silveree. 'If I could applaud, I would!'

A polite round of applause was readily given. Silveree cheered in the background while Cyril fluttered athletically.

'Laugh as much as you like but I've got to perfect this fuel or we're not - or should I say Bardee isn't - going anywhere,' Tien haughtily retorted. 'I have a new batch ready for testing.'

'Marvellous,' grinned Silveree. 'Shall we see how it works?'

They all trooped into Tien's lab and watched the preparations. A pipe protruding from the wall fed liquid into a large vat. A burner was pushed under the vat and the incoming liquid was heated until it formed a gas. As it boiled, Tien placed a glass cone over the top. The gas flowed through the cone along a tube before dropping into a flask. When the flask was full Tien put a cork in the top and put it on the table. Placing a pair of goggles over his eyes, he picked up a long taper.

'Now, if my calculations are correct I should be able to light the gas and it will burn slowly thus giving the Nepo forward thrust.'

As he went to light the taper Nabi, Bardee and Merly threw themselves behind the upturned table, covering their ears. Seeing his friend's reaction, Cyril took off and hid behind some books. Unaware of any potential danger, Eric stood and watched. Taking a keen interest, Silveree hovered behind Tien who held the lit taper over the flask and removed the cork. There was a blinding flash, followed by an enormous explosion. The blast threw Eric backwards, high in the air. On and on he soared until coming down with a wallop on top of the three wary sheep behind the table. Untangling their various limbs, they peered nervously over the table's edge.

Silveree, completely unharmed, with a strange smile playing across his face, hadn't moved. Tien, however, had! He looked as if he'd been stuck to the wall at least eight feet off the floor with all four legs outstretched. His face was blackened; smoke wafted out of his smouldering hair. He wore an expression of amazement, shock, confusion and fear all mixed into one. There was no sign of his goggles, just two white circles where they once had been. Unsticking, he slowly slid down the wall. His hind legs crumpled beneath him as he hit the floor. The downward journey ended with him sitting open mouthed and cross-legged on the ground. Composure returned, Eric rushed to his friend's aid.

'Are you alright!?' he asked.

Whilst Tien's mouth did open and close, no words came out. Blankly, he stared at Eric. Frayed nerves recovered, the others gathered round.

'Get some water!' said Eric.

A bucket of ice cold water was handed to Eric who threw it over the unfortunate scientist. Seconds passed before they noticed any effect, then Tien screamed and shot back up the wall nearly as high as he'd been blown before coming back to earth with a thump. Concerned friends helped him to his feet. Water flew everywhere as the blackened boffin shook himself dry.

'Interesting, most interesting,' he said. 'A little more work I feel.'

Still feeling the effects of the disastrous experiment, he staggered off uncertainly to continue his quest for Nepo fuel.

Meanwhile, Silveree had been studying the contents of the vat and looking at all the chemical bottles that lined the walls.

'Would you care to have another go, my sizzled chum?' he asked Tien.

'No way brother, I'm outta here!' exclaimed Merly.

'I'm gone!' said Nabi.

'Oh ye sheep of little faith!' Silveree retorted.

'Come on then,' Bardee said.' We have to get that crate in the air!'

'Very well,' said a wobbly Tien.

Gathering round to watch, a hush fell upon the reluctant audience.

The glass cone had been blown into the corner of the lab. Tien retrieved it and went to place it back on the vat when Silveree coughed. He pointedly stared at a bottle on a shelf until Tien realised what he was doing. With the aid of a chair Tien retrieved the bottle, uncorked it and was about to pour the contents into the vat. Silveree had an immediate coughing fit and gestured Tien towards the flask that by some miracle had survived the blast and was still sitting there. Singing loudly, Silveree smiled contentedly as the chemical was poured into the flask. As soon as there was enough, he coughed again. Pouring stopped immediately and the glass tube was reinserted.

Soon the experiment was ready. Burner relit, they watched the gas pour into the chemical filled flask. Silveree spluttered and the cork was immediately inserted. Taper lit, Tien was about to remove the cork when Silveree coughed again! Astonished, Tien saw his friend shaking like a jelly and making vibrating noises. Then the penny dropped. He picked up the flask and shook it vigorously. Enthralled, they watched the chemical slowly dissolve into the gas, forming a blue cloud.

Placing the flask back on the table, he picked up the lit taper and made ready to repeat the process when there was a flurry of activity around him. Fearing the worst, his audience's nerve had broken. They had all fled behind the table again, Eric included!

'Umphh!' Tien said.

Cork removed, he nervously held the taper at arm's length, slowly edging it over the top of the flask. When it got there he closed his eyes, hoping for the best. There was a slight pop as the mixture ignited, followed by a roaring sound. Upon opening his eyes he beheld an amazing sight! Blue flames were shooting skyward. Such were the forces being produced, the flask was slowly being pushed through the table! Vibrations became stronger and stronger. Four nervous heads appeared, looking on in amazement. The noise reached a deafening crescendo before the flask burst right through! Accelerating wildly, it glanced off the floor and tore across the lab, spewing flames from its neck. Within a microsecond it had reached the speed of sound, roaring over the four awestruck heads before burying itself deep into the wall behind them with a last belch of flame and ear bending roar.

Blue smoke filled the cave. The silence was deafening. They all gathered round the smouldering hole in the wall, stunned and amazed. No one spoke for several minutes.

'Wow! Brothers, I mean wow!' cried Merly.

'I thought I was fast!' exclaimed Nabi.

'When can you fuel her up?' asked Bardee, eyes glazed with excitement.

'Well done!' Eric shouted.

'As I said, all it needed was a little more work,' Tien casually remarked.

Nerves shredded, Cyril had fled outside, vowing never to return if anyone was going to light anything.

CHAPTER 11

RUNWAYS & TEST FLIGHTS

Life transformed, Bardee spent his time inspecting the Nepo and playing with the controls. Nights were spent dreaming of the time he could defy gravity in his beloved machine. He soared to great heights, jinking left, right, swooping low and waving to his friends before hurtling vertically skywards, disappearing from sight, reaching for the stars. Every morning they were fresh in his mind, making him more impatient than ever for the momentous day to arrive.

The test flight wasn't far away now. Gallons of fuel had been prepared and Tien had been tinkering with the bell jars. All was ready when an awful thought struck Bardee. So involved had he been with the Nepo he hadn't thought of one thing, a thing as necessary as his winged machine itself. A runway! He hadn't seen a runway! The Nepo was useless without one! Panic stricken, he tore off to see Tien. Tien listened to his friend before calmly reassuring him. When everyone was gathered together the scientist led them to the other side of the giant cliff that Eric had seen on his arrival. Stretching away into the distance, shimmering in the sunlight, was a flat stretch of land the width of two Nepos. Elephants, with leaf covered branches grasped in their trunks, were sweeping it flat. Smaller animals were picking up little stones, then depositing them in the forest on either side. Lions and tigers patrolled the perimeter.

Joy uncontained, Bardee tore down the runway, inspecting everything in his path. Soon he was just an ever changing shape as the heat haze played tricks with their eyes before disappearing into the distant horizon. Minutes passed before he slowly reappeared, dreamlike and distorted. As he came ever nearer the yellow strip on his wool looked like it was blowing in the wind, streaming skywards behind him. Suddenly, he burst back into reality, stopping in front of his friends, tired but elated. He stared back down the runway before turning to them, grinning from ear to ear.

'It's alive! My dream's alive! We can do it! This is perfect, couldn't be better!' he panted. 'All I need is a flag. I have to know the wind direction!

'That's easy, brother!' Merly laughed as he ran off.

'How long have the animals been working on this?' asked Eric.

'Not long,' said Tien. 'At one time there were hundreds of them, whole herds of elephants, lions, tigers and all sorts. They know how desperate things are.'

'The burning is getting closer,' growled Nabi.

Time was running out and Eric knew it.

'Can we test fly the Nepo tomorrow?' he asked.

Tien looked at Silveree, who nodded.

'Yes!' he replied unerringly.

Flag held aloft, Merly returned! Fluttering gently in the breeze, Eric saw its detail for the first time.

Across the flag with Tien in the middle were portraits of all their heads, Eric's included. Poor Arbe was there too. Along the bottom it said: 'SPECIAL SHEEP AREN'T SCARED.'

'How simply, simply marvellous!' exclaimed Silveree. 'A worthy flag indeed!'

'And people think all I can do is sing,' Merly said immodestly.

Taking the flag from Merly, the would-be airman ran to the edge of the runway and planted the flagpole in the ground. Obligingly, the flag continued its fluttering.

The day of the test flight dawned. Desperate to get in the air, Bardee's night had been restless. Over and over in his mind he went through all he had to do. Perhaps there were things he didn't know. If so, would he learn them in time or perhaps crash? Test pilots are made of stern stuff, he decided, and all would come good!

A hearty breakfast was prepared for him along with much support from the others. Tien fussed around the Nepo, making last minute adjustments under the watchful eye of Silveree. Finally, the moment arrived! Elephants pushed the rocks away from the cliff face. There, in the shadows, lurked the mighty Nepo! The group stood around the huge beast, waiting for the test pilot.

At last he emerged, wearing a look of calm resolution. The yellow strip on his wool blew about wildly, burning the brightest yellow imaginable. Ladder in place, he was about to climb into the cockpit, when Eric said, 'I'm coming with you!'

'I thought this might happen,' said Tien. 'If you must, you have to wear one of these.'

He handed Eric a large material bundle with two straps hanging off it.

'What is it?' he asked.

'A puchatera.'

'What's it for?'

Tien helped Eric get his front legs through the straps before tightening them across his chest. After a struggle they got the bundle sitting comfortably on his back. A cord hung down the front.

'I found six of them in one of the caves. If the Nepo's going to crash you must jump out and pull the cord,' he said. 'If the images on the cave walls are right you'll float slowly down to the ground. I've five left. I took one to pieces to see how it worked.'

'I don't want one of those,' said Bardee

Eric climbed the ladder and sat down. Bardee was about to follow when Merly stopped him.

'Brother, I've made you these.'

He handed Bardee a helmet made of leather with two holes cut in the top to accommodate his ears and a pair of goggles. They embraced emotionally. Having placed the helmet on his head and adjusted the chinstrap, he pulled the goggles over his eyes, boarded the Nepo, strapped himself in and prepared for take-off.

Taper in hand, Tien stood under the Nepo, ready to light the engines. Controls adjusted, Bardee gave the thumbs up. The taper was raised behind the first bell jar. There was a cough followed by a roar as it burst into life. Immediately, the other was lit with the same result. Bardee increased the power. Flames from the bell jars filled the sky and noise rent the air. More thrust was applied, pushing the Nepo slowly out of the cave.

Gently lining the monster up with the runway, he applied full power. The blast from the engines nearly blew the anxious scientist off his feet. The noise was almost unbearable. Inexorably the Nepo lumbered forward, slowly at first but gradually increasing speed. Bardee surveyed his instruments; all seemed well but was the runway long enough? Halfway down it now he knew he needed a lot more speed. He pushed the throttles forward as far as he could without breaking them. The Nepo, surging forward, seemed as keen to get in the air as he was. Faster still the Nepo went as they thundered down the runway. They were at the end now. Trees raced towards them as Bardee desperately pulled back on the stick. Slowly, oh so slowly, the great machine lumbered into the air. Branches reached out for the Nepo as it clawed its way over the trees, breaking twigs as it lurched into the sky. Then they were clear, climbing slowly into a clear sky. Sheer delight filled Bardee's heart as he experimented with the controls, banking right, left, climbing, descending, even gliding with the throttles closed! Never had he felt so free! Now the Nepo was speeding along he closed the throttles slightly and they both enjoyed the view. Forests, plains and mountains hurtled beneath them. Animals looked up in amazement. Fortunately, there was no sign of any Nokemys. Eric signalled that they should return. Bardee changed course and the monster obeyed, winging its way home. Anxiously, Tien and company stared skywards.

'I hear them!' exclaimed Nabi.

A faint hum could be heard in the distance. Soon they could see a tiny dot, high in the sky, growing ever larger and louder.

Slowly, the Nepo descended towards the landing strip. Full of confidence, Bardee decided to do a fly-past. Lining up the Nepo with the runway, he applied full power and sped down it towards his waiting friends. Halfway along it his fighter pilot side got the better of him and he flipped the Nepo upside down! A strapless Eric, who until that moment had been thoroughly enjoying himself, frantically tried to hang on. Gravity took over, shooting him out of the plane, hurling him earthwards. Safely strapped into his seat, Bardee looked down in horror as his friend disappeared from view.

Speeding towards the ground, Eric desperately tried to collect his thoughts. Pull the cord! Pull the cord! After a second's panic he found it and gave it a hefty tug. The bundle on his back opened, pushing out a silk cloth that slowly expanded into an umbrella shape before a strong jerk on his shoulders told him he was slowing down. Below him, he could see the upturned faces of his anxious friends. Touching down gently, he managed to stay on his feet. The Nepo landed and a distraught Bardee rushed over.

'I'm so sorry, dear Eric, will you ever forgive me?' he cried.

'Forgive you? There's nothing to forgive! Our plan is now complete!' laughed Eric.

Everyone congratulated everyone else. Bardee was hoisted on Nabi and Merly's shoulders and carried triumphantly into the Nepo cave.

Exhilarated by all he'd seen, Silveree said 'I don't think I've had this much excitement in four billion years!'

Now, thought Eric, with a wry smile, the serious planning can begin.

CHAPTER 12

THE PLAN UNFOLDS

Eric knew what had to be done. How to do it was the problem. Nothing must be left to chance. All the pieces were there. Just put them together, he thought! Hour after hour he puzzled, until finally the jigsaw fell into place. A meeting was called.

'We go tomorrow night,' Eric said. 'This is the plan. The Nepo is too noisy to get close. We'd lose the element of surprise. So we're going to use puchateras. Bardee, you glide the Nepo over the Facility. We'll drop in unheard and unseen. All this has to be done at night, with no moon. It's difficult but I know we can do it. Nabi, you come with me to the genetic mix room and help me make the switch. Merly, you keep lookout. Cyril, you can be our eyes and ears. Tien says the genetic mix takes two days to work so we have to stay hidden on the roof until then. If all goes to plan and the new batch of our brothers and sisters arrive we have to complete the Hopsons' nasty surprise. How we do that depends on circumstances at the time.

Bardee, if you get the signal, land the Nepo in the Facility. Remember, no violence. If we fail, we're all finished. Any questions?'

Cyril was going to say something but seeing his medal, his courage returned.

Addressing them from above, Silveree said, 'A most enterprising and cunning plan. I shall be there with you and do what little I can to help. You are indeed a most special band of brothers.'

'Band of Brothers!' Merly exclaimed. 'Now that's a vibe I can get along with.'

They all nodded in agreement.

Silveree glowed silently above them, before continuing. 'You are about to embark upon this great plan, toward which you have worked so hard. The hopes and prayers of all the animals march with you. Your task is not an easy one but victory will bring an end to tyranny, leaving you all to live in peace and prosperity.'

Stunned into silence, they all looked at him before breaking into loud cheers.

Eric smiled at him, 'Thank you Silveree, you are a true friend!'

Tien spent the night locked in his lab. Much hammering, drilling and welding was heard. Dawn broke to find them summoned by a tired scientist. The gadget cupboard door was open, strange objects littered the table.

'I have some things that may help you on your mission,' said Tien.

Picking up a long piece of rope with a loop on the end, he was about to say something when Merly interrupted him.

'What are we supposed to do with that, hang ourselves?'

Nervous laughter rippled quietly around the cave.

'That's not funny. I never joke about my work!' Tien replied sternly. 'This is to loop round the genetic mix jar to help you lift it out of the room. Notice, it has knots all the way up to help Nabi grip it.'

'Good idea!' said Eric.

'Also here is a harness for you to wear, Eric. A rope fixes to the back so Nabi can lower you down. Notice, it also has knots to aid grip.'

He picked up a little pipe shaped thing. 'Now this is really good. If you press the button at the end, it fires a poison dart. This will render whoever it hits unconscious for ten minutes but will do them no lasting harm. Notice, please, that is has a safety catch, here.' He pointed to a little hook on the side. 'So hopefully, you won't shoot yourselves!'

Lastly, picking up two objects shaped like candles, he said, 'These are flares: one marked red, the other green. When you pull the tab on the top it will release a cloud of smoke. Use it for signalling Bardee: green to land, red to stay away. Notice, it can also be used as a smokescreen, thus hiding your whereabouts.'

'Marvellous, my dear fellow,' cried Silveree. 'You really have thought of everything!'

Clouded by their sombre mood, the day passed slowly. They whiled away the hours talking, dozing, eating and writing letters. Eric put his amongst the piles of books in the hope that one day someone might find it and read their story. Time dragged on, until at last zero hour approached.

Merly cried, 'It's time for a song!'

He jumped on the table and sang 'I think I got those pre op blues!'

'When I woke up this morning
I couldn't believe my ears
They were big, white and woolly
Could do with a snip from the shears
We have to look the business

For the all important days ahead
Our equipment must be polished
And maybe helmets on our head
Oh yes, we sure got those pre-op blues

We have all our gear at the ready
Assembled carefully piece by piece
I think that my brand new puchatera
Was made from my very own fleece
Our training is meticulous
I believe it's the best in the book
We once tried out a shepherd
But he was a bit of a crook
Oh yes, we sure got those pre-op blues

Freedom is the keyword
For the vital job in hand
Get in, get out, no flocking about
Just as our leader planned
This is really what we live for
The mission, success and home
One for all and all for one
Feeling that we're never a clone
Oh yes, we sure got those pre-op blues'

The mood was broken! Rapturous cheering broke out!

Finally, the hour had come. Merly strode out onto the runway with the flag.

'What d'you think brothers?' he asked, pointing at the flag.

On the back he'd added in large gold letters the words 'THE WOOLLY JUMPERS.' Underneath was a painting of the Nepo with Bardee at the controls and three puchaterists heading earthwards.

'Couldn't be better,' smiled Eric.

'Now that's a flag to raise the spirits,' said Bardee, proudly.

'Well done!' added Tien.

Nabi patted Merly on the back but said nothing. He already had his mission face on.

'My dear fellow, an act of genius, how utterly marvellous!' beamed Silveree.

When the excitement had died down, they strapped neatly packed rucksacks onto their chests. Tien helped them into their puchateras. Filled with emotion, they said farewell to their mentor and oldest friend. One by one, they climbed into the Nepo, steeling themselves for what lay ahead. Final checks completed, Bardee manoeuvred onto the runway. Lights twinkled down its length, converging to a point in the far distant darkness. Animals of every kind stood either side of it, hopeful eyes fixed upon the Nepo and its occupants. Upon seeing this, the full weight of responsibility fell heavily upon them all. This was their only chance and everyone knew it. Full power was applied with a deafening roar; sheets of flame pursued the Nepo as it surged down the runway, eventually disappearing into the night sky, leaving behind a crushing silence. Taking one last look at his disappearing friends, Tien, heart full of sadness and hope, walked slowly back to his lab. Silveree hovered dimly before disappearing into the night. The animals melted away into the forest.

Take off had been easier the second time round and the Nepo thundered higher into the night sky. Since the plan had been hatched, Merly had a nasty feeling that flying wasn't his thing and now in the air he knew it! He'd even contemplated jumping out whilst the Nepo was still on the runway but loyalty to his friends had overcome his initial fear. Now, high in the air, blind terror had taken over! If sheep were supposed to fly they'd have wings, he thought as he cowered on the floor, eyes closed. Nabi, if he was afraid, didn't show it. Up front, pilot and navigator kept a look out for the Facility. Height was what they needed to avoid being heard on the ground, so they flew round in circles, gaining altitude at every turn. Below them they saw the forest fires burning, tightening their grip on all they knew and loved. The flames of determination in Eric's heart grew stronger than the blaze below. After an hour the engines started to cough, letting Bardee know they could go no higher.

The Nepo was levelled out before heading for the drop zone. Soon they saw its sickly, silver light in the distant darkness. Throttles closed, utterly silent, the Nepo started its descent. A red light was turned on to warn the puchaterists to be ready. Nabi and Eric sat on the edge of the cockpit, staring nervously down into the black abyss. Putting a reassuring leg around the terrified singer, Eric helped him up there with them. Wind and airspeed judged to perfection, Bardee flicked on the 'green for go' light. Nabi jumped immediately, leaving the terrified Merly with Eric who had to pull his unwilling friend off with him, hanging onto him as they fell. Nabi pulled his cord. From Eric's point of view he seemed to shoot upwards as his puchatera took effect. Petrified, Merly was never going to do anything. Struggling frantically with his rigid friend until he found the cord, Eric pulled it hard before letting him go. Now the roof was getting ever larger as he plummeted earthwards. Hoping that there was time for his own puchatera to work, Eric pulled his cord. The roof flew up to meet him at break neck speed and he landed with a terrific thump. He lay still for a while, getting his breath back whilst watching Nabi land close by. Such was Merly's terror that he hadn't opened his eyes since his ghastly fall had begun and he landed in a heap with his puchatera falling on top of him, forming a tent over his head. Finally, he opened his eyes to see nothing but blackness.

'So this is it, I'm on my way to sheep brother heaven,' he whimpered.

Eric, now recovered, reached him first and pulled the puchatera off him. Wide, white eyes stared blankly into the distance. Eventually, he snapped out of his trance and looked at Eric.

'Am I?' he stammered. 'Are we still alive?'

'Of course we're alive!' laughed Eric.

Relief began to flood his face; he leapt to his feet and embraced Eric. 'Never, never, never again!' he said. 'If that's fun, I can't sing! That fly boy has gotta be crazy!'

'Takes all sorts,' grinned Nabi softly.

Puchateras were removed and hidden under some loose roof tiles. They sat for a while, allowing Merly to recover before taking in what they were going to do next. Above them, the Nepo glided away into the far distance before Bardee restarted the engines then climbed unheard into the night sky.

Several feet below them Generalissimo was ecstatic; a batch of sheep had been through the Facility trouble free. So great was his pleasure that he'd decided to issue a medal to himself in recognition of his greatness. On the gallery floor a guard of honour was lined up, waiting for him. Stood at the end of the line was Toady with the most enormous gold medal, laid on a red velvet cushion. The guard was composed of White Mask and three of his associates; the rest were Nokemys. As the lift doors were flung open the guard of honour leapt to attention and Generalissimo Walter Strumphh strutted forward in all his glory. His powder blue cylindrical hat was at a more rakish angle than usual and the medals on his chest were so brightly polished they hurt Toady's eyes. He flounced past the guards, giving them a disdainful look before wobbling to a halt in front of his assistant.

Toady had written a short speech in his honour and was about to wax lyrical when Generalissimo grabbed the medal from the cushion and tried to put it around his fat neck. This proved troublesome because of his tall hat, fat body and short arms. Try as he might, he couldn't get his latest award over the top of the cylinder and he ended up bent double, desperately trying to reach the top of the hat that was now touching the floor! The unequal struggle continued for a while until he finally stood up with his headgear pushed down over his eyes, still at a rakish angle, with the medal dangling precariously from the very peak of his garish garb. After much struggling, sweating and swearing, plus not inconsiderable help from White Mask, the feat was finally accomplished. Dignity nearly restored, he pushed White Mask contemptuously aside and strode over to the Gallery window in time to see the last few sheep trickling meekly towards the door at the end of the hall. Smug conceit filled his whole being as he surveyed the culmination of his work.

He turned to address his guard of honour. 'I have awarded myself an even higher award than the highest possible award I have already awarded myself. The previous highest award could never be a high enough award for the achievements I have achieved over the past week. My genius has reached plains hitherto untouched by my previous genius. Look before you!' he cried. 'No more renegades; a sea of untroubled wealth for me and my kingdom!'

They all looked down to see the last sheep disappear into the tunnel. White Mask was looking pleased with himself.

Generalissimo saw this and stalked over to him, spitting into his face, 'Be grateful you're alive. Remember, one more mistake and you won't be!' Turning to Toady and the Nokemys, 'Reduce the guard! Use them to increase the burning even more. They must have no place to hide. I want those sheep dead or alive.' A look of delicious wickedness spewed across his hideous features. 'Preferably roasted alive!'

At that, he waddled into the lift. Roasted sheep had a certain appeal to Toady. He tried to control his dribbling with vile thoughts about his master but a nice leg of lamb was too much to bear. Small, sticky drops fell onto the front of his suit, forming a yellow crust. The group stood there looking down at the huge empty room whilst contemplating their own futures.

Back on the roof, Merly was his normal self again. Cyril, medal round his neck, had summoned all his remaining courage and joined them. Not wanting to go back inside, Eric suggested he stayed where he was and keep lookout. Overjoyed, Cyril sat importantly on the highest part of the roof, keenly surveying all around him. The three sheep checked their map of the Facility and organised their equipment before quietly removing the grill Cyril had squeezed through. Silently, Eric, Merly and Nabi dropped into the tunnel. They crawled quickly along to the grating in the corridor where Merly stayed whilst the other two went quietly on to the genetic mix room. Slowly, silently, they removed the metal plate and stared down at the jar below them.

'It's a long way down!' whispered Eric.

'I can handle it,' replied Nabi, opening his rucksack and unfurling a rope that he connected to the clip on Eric's harness. They knew one mistake and it was over. Carefully, Eric sat on the edge of the gaping hole and Nabi handed him an empty jar. The rope was pulled taut and Eric let himself slide off into thin air. Bracing himself against the wall, Nabi slowly played the rope out, gradually lowering

Eric towards his destination. Even for a sheep of his enormous strength it was difficult. He was grateful for the knots Tien had tied in it.

All was going well. Eric was halfway down when Nabi heard Merly whisper, 'Get him up quick, someone's coming!'

Frantically, he pulled sharply on the rope. Eric, who had heard nothing, was suddenly jerked violently upwards, losing his grip on the jar. As it fell away, he made a frantic grab at it, managing to catch it by the rim but only just! He could feel his grip on it fading away. Desperately, he reached for it. The jar was about to plummet to the floor when he managed to get a leg underneath it and clutch it gratefully to his chest. Now he heard voices and knew what was happening. Nabi heaved on the rope for all he was worth and Eric sped back towards the ceiling. The door below opened as he neared the grating. Nabi stopped pulling and Eric, heart pounding, hardly daring to breathe, hung motionless in the air above Generalissimo, White Mask and Toady.

The three of them stood silently, inspecting the seal on the genetic mix jar. White Mask made final checks on the connections before they all stood back, admiring their handiwork.

'All's well, Generalissimo! The formula is perfected and the mix is untouched,' said White Mask.

'It had better be!' hissed Strumphh. 'Or for you and your kind the consequences are unthinkable!' He pointed at Toady. 'That goes for you too!'

'Yes master,' grovelled Toady, taking a fearful step away from his boss.

'I guarantee it,' replied White Mask, the confidence in his voice hiding an underlying nervousness.

'Excellent,' Strumphh replied. 'How long before the process starts?'

'Two hours,' replied White Mask. They opened the door and filed out.

Eric's heart slowed down with the relief of seeing them leave. He'd never seen the creatures that were trying to destroy their world before. Sensing the fear felt by White Mask and Toady, he almost felt sorry for them. He knew instinctively that the creature in blue was indeed a deadly adversary. The task before them seemed more daunting than ever. This was not the time for wavering; he signalled Nabi to start lowering him again. Merly had been watching Nabi and could see that even with his great strength he was beginning to struggle. He'd been holding Eric for over five minutes now and the strain was beginning to tell. Merly decided that it was more important to help Nabi than keep watch. Along the thin corridor he crept, grabbing the end of the rope and taking the strain. A surprised Nabi turned to him and smiled. The rope was played out and Eric descended towards the floor. He signalled them to stop when he reached the jar. Slowly swaying in the air he carefully pulled out the two tubes attached to the mix, undid the seal and poured the contents of the jar into the one he was holding.

Nabi turned to Merly, 'I've got him, send down the rope.'

Merly let Nabi take the strain, took the looped rope out of Nabi's rucksack and lowered it down. Eric put the rope around the jar and drew it tight. Merly slowly pulled it up to the grating and grabbed it. With great care he looped the rope round Tien's genetic mix then carefully lowered it down to the swaying Eric.

'Hurry up,' groaned Nabi, 'I can't hold him much longer.'

Merly looked at him. He was beginning to tremble with the strain. Never had he seen the torches on his coat burn so fiercely! As fast as possible, Eric poured in Tien's mix, replaced the seal and the two tubes before signalling all was well. He could feel Nabi's distress by the vibrations through his rope harness. Merly took as much of the strain on the rope as he could. Together they slowly heaved Eric back up. Merly could hear Nabi's breathing getting heavier and heavier as exhaustion set in. Summoning the last strength available to both of them, they pulled for all they were worth and Eric appeared in the mouth of the grating. Merly grabbed the jar and pulled him through. Nabi immediately collapsed to the floor in a state of semi consciousness. He'd given everything and was having trouble breathing. His heart was pounding so fast that Eric and Merly could hear it thrashing wildly in his chest. The torches on his sides had become duller. They sat there looking at him for a while, hoping he'd breathe normally but nothing seemed to change.

'Nabi brother, we need you,' pleaded Merly quietly.

A few seconds passed before Nabi opened his eyes, 'I'm not done yet,' he gasped, 'Not until I've found Arbe!' He paused for a second, looking at Merly. 'Thanks brother, I couldn't have done it without you.'

Such was Merly's joy that he embraced the prostrate athlete. Nabi looked up at him, smiling, 'Now get off, we got things to do.'

'There's a song in there somewhere!' laughed Merly.

As they slowly recovered, their coats shone fiercely again. Eric had never seen the notes on Merly's dance so bright and fast. Nabi lay there, breathing normally again, fiery torches flickering in the half-light of the corridor. Whilst waiting for Nabi to recover fully, Eric replaced the grating. When all was done they slowly made their way back to the roof. As they emerged, Cyril looked anxious but their smiles turned his concerns to joy! Such was his pleasure at seeing them, he gave a flying display of such breathtaking skill they had to force themselves into not applauding and giving the game away!

Cyril had nothing to report, so the four of them settled down for the long wait ahead. They ate some of the food Tien had prepared and lay in the sunshine, talking quietly amongst themselves. Cyril, exhausted after his aerial acrobatics, was asleep in seconds, snoring loudly.

As darkness swept in, the Facility regained its sickly aura; all that could be heard was the quiet hum of machinery. Eric couldn't sleep. His mind was full of what lay ahead. If the mix switch didn't work, nothing mattered. If it did, what would they do next? The Facility had to be explored in detail, he decided. Merly woke with a start to see Eric standing over him. He listened as his friend told him that if he didn't come back, under no circumstances were they to come looking for him. They must get on with the plan as best they could. Merly tried to argue but to no avail, Eric would have none of it. Having helped him into his rucksack Merly watched Eric climb down the shaft, waiting until he'd disappeared from sight before returning to his slumbers.

CHAPTER 13

THE FACILITY

Carefully picking his way through the maze of thin corridors that fed through the ceilings of the Facility, Eric came across pipes that snaked everywhere, feeding cool air to the various rooms that passed under his feet. Below him, creatures worked at various experiments and wrote things in books. Guards were on duty everywhere. Revisiting the genetic mix room, he saw that the process had begun. Fluids were coursing through the mix jar and out through the wall. All their futures depended upon what was happening in that room. Blanking the thought from his mind, he carried on; dwelling on it only pushed him away from the job in hand. The plan would work and they had to be as ready as they could be. Up until now, what he really wanted to find had eluded him; the huge room where he had started his journey. Not wanting to get lost, he left some of his wool at every corner. As soon as it left his body the bright colours disappeared immediately.

Carrying on down the endless tunnels, he eventually turned a corner to be confronted by a dead end. He looked up and saw a steel ladder that seemed to climb endlessly straight upwards. Knowing the huge room had a very high ceiling, he hoped this might take him to it. Pulling himself up the shaft, he started up the ladder. After ten minutes of an exhausting climb he reached the top, where there was another shaft leading away to the right. Slowly edging his way down it, he eventually arrived at another grating in the floor. Horrible memories flooded back. There, way below, was the huge, terrible room. An uncontrollable shudder of fear leapt through him. Quickly regaining his composure, he thought about how they'd get down to the floor. I wish I'd brought Nabi with me: he'd have known, Eric thought. Continuing along the corridor, he came to another tunnel, branching away into the distance. Eric guessed that this one led to the black glass fronted room. Quickly making his way down it, he reached yet another grating. He was right; there beneath him was the room that overlooked the sea of sheep. Now he knew where he wanted to be, the problem was how to get down. Having seen all that was necessary he made his way back to the ladder. I need to get back quickly, he thought: we've a lot of planning to do. Pushing himself into the shaft, he started to descend the ladder as fast as possible. Climbing rhythmically down gave him time to think. Plans, ideas, some mad, some sensible, charged round his head, making it fit to burst. So engrossed was he that he'd stopped thinking about the ladder and missed his footing on a rung, causing him to tip backwards into the air. Frantically clutching for the ladder, he started to fall. The floor hurtled towards him. Closing his eyes, he waited for the end. Everything had slowed down in his mind: all his adventures flashed by, but most of all the disappointment of letting his friends down. Suddenly, something clutched at the straps on his rucksack. His fall was stopped in such a bone jarring way that his eyes nearly popped out of their sockets.

It took a few seconds for what had happened to sink in. Eric looked around in amazement. He was facing the wall with the ladder behind him, hanging in the air, some fifty feet from the bottom of the shaft; something had caught in his rucksack. Struggling to turn around to free himself, he quickly realised it was impossible.

Whatever he was caught on was beyond his reach. He was stuck there, with no hope of getting down. Dangling there helplessly, he considered his options: if he took his rucksack off the fall could kill him. Even if he survived, they were bound to hear the thump as he hit the ceiling. Worse still, he could go straight through the floor and be captured. None were sensible options. If only he'd brought Nabi with him none of this would have happened. How stupid I've been, he thought. Helplessly hanging there, time dragged by. He worried about his friends. Anger coursed through his veins. Personal vanity had got in the way of common sense. He may be a leader but now he knew he couldn't do everything himself. Despair overcame him at the realisation that he'd learnt this lesson too late.

Falling into an uneasy sleep, strange dreams buffeted him. He seemed outside of himself, looking in. The head of the monstrous creature in the blue uniform towered above him, tongue forked like a serpent. The hideous spectre laughed at him as he cowered in the corner of the room, his coat shining colourfully one minute and turning a dull white the next. The more the monster laughed, the duller the white became. He dreamt of his friends, walking away into darkness as the vile vision flicked putrid balls of venom from its snake tongue at them. Upon hitting them, the colour immediately drained from their coats. Eric, powerless to intervene, watched helplessly as this horrible scene unfolded in front of him, repeating itself over and over.

Waking with a jump, Eric heard something beneath him. Hanging there helplessly, his spirits sank as the noise came ever nearer. Just short of the shaft the noise stopped. Now the only sound was his thumping heart. The noise began again and someone appeared in the shaft below. It was Nabi!

He bounded up the ladder and with his enormous strength lifted Eric off the hook that had caught his rucksack strap. Carefully this time, Eric descended the ladder, embracing Nabi at the bottom.

'Merly tried to stop me but something told me you needed help,' said Nabi.

'Never have I been so pleased to see you. I thought it was all over for me.'

'Don't go off on your own,' Nabi said curtly. 'We're all in this together.'

'You're right. That's a mistake I will never make again.

'Good,' said Nabi.

'Now you're here, let me show you what I've found.'

They both went up the ladder, retracing Eric's steps before making their way safely back to the roof where an anxious Merly and Cyril were waiting.

Merly leapt joyously to his feet as they pulled themselves onto the roof. Eric explained his adventures and mishaps - then they finalised their plans. Tomorrow was the big day and they had to be in position early. Nabi wanted to look for Arbe immediately but Eric said no. He'd be too angry and take unnecessary risks; his time would come for that. Nabi didn't like it but with further persuasion from Merly, he finally agreed. His job was to drop down on a rope into the huge room and rally the sheep. Eric was going to do the same into the glass room and deal with whatever came along. Merly had a free role that he felt befitted a creative soul such as his and would do whatever he thought necessary to help the others. Eric asked Cyril if he'd come inside and be their go-between. Cyril panicked at the thought but was reassured that he could go with Eric and burrow inside his coat until needed. Cyril sincerely hoped he'd never be needed as his courage was running out, if it hadn't run out already. Gripping his medal tightly, he reluctantly agreed. Part of him wished he was just an ordinary butterfly, flitting about the forest, but once a superhero, always a superhero. This thought cheered him up no end and soon he was fast asleep.

Eating and resting was essential. Tomorrow they all hoped their plan would come to fruition, allowing peace and harmony to reign. As dusk fell on the Facility, all that could be heard was the loud snoring of a butterfly mingled with the gentle whispers of the little group before sleep eased them away.

The weather was fine as they awoke on the morning of the fateful day. They ate the rest of the food and checked their equipment before helping each other into their rucksacks. Nabi hoped the rope was long enough to get him to the floor of the enormous room: otherwise he'd have to jump and take his chances; but if anyone could do it, he could, and nothing, but nothing, was going to stop him in his quest to find dear Arbe. The little group emotionally bade farewell to each other before disappearing through the grating. Cyril had never burrowed so deeply into Eric's coat and he felt secure, for the moment at least.

Back at the cave, Tien and Bardee were beside themselves with worry. Neither could settle or do anything. Both of them had tinkered endlessly with the Nepo. They'd refuelled it, then double checked their double checking. Now they felt helpless. On more than one occasion, Tien had to stop Bardee from flying over the Facility to see what was going on. Bardee knew he was right but was desperate to do something positive. Tien paced endlessly up and down, looking older by the minute. Bardee tried reading books but couldn't concentrate.

At last the day arrived and they went over everything again. At least it passed the time. They tried to eat but couldn't. Bardee put on his flying hat and goggles. This normally cheered him up no end, but not on this occasion. Tien tried some new experiments but his heart wasn't in it. He didn't even manage to blow himself up, which in some bizarre way disappointed him.

The hour was approaching when Tien dropped a bombshell!

'I'm coming with you.'

Bardee had been trying to read a book, which wasn't easy through his goggles. He dropped it in shock.

'No you're not, you're too -' he stopped himself before he said the word.

'Old, you mean,' said Tien.

'Well,' he paused for a second. 'Yes, you are too old. You know what Eric said.'

'I don't care what Eric said. I can't stay here doing nothing.'

'But you might be needed here afterwards,' reasoned Bardee.

'There won't be an afterwards if this doesn't work. I'm coming and that's that!'

Bardee could see that arguing was pointless. There was one condition though: Tien had to wear the last puchatera. The scientist needed no convincing and they sat together, waiting for the time to take off.

CHAPTER 14

THE LAST THROW OF THE DICE

Silveree hadn't been seen for a while; so intent were the band of brothers on their mission, they'd half-forgotten him. Low his profile may have been but he was looking after them. All their struggles passed under his watchful gaze. He'd dropped Nabi the hint about Eric's plight on the ladder. Silveree hoped he'd get away with it. That didn't count as interfering as far as he was concerned and so far so good. Silently, invisibly he watched their every move.

They each made their way quietly to their appointed positions with Merly prowling to and fro between his two comrades. Nabi, rope by his side, peered intently down into the white, empty vastness below him. Eric waited patiently above the glass room.

Time seemed to stand still; hours passed with nothing happening. Eric's nerves were becoming frayed. Was it going to plan? Was something wrong? Now, one way or the other he just wanted it over with. At last, the lift door of the glass room burst open and in strutted

Generalissimo with his two cronies. Eric knew the moment they'd been waiting for was nearly upon them. By craning his neck through the grating, he could just see into the vast room beyond. It was still empty.

Nabi's pent-up energy was getting the better of him. Sitting around was never his strong suit and the suspense was unbearable. For the hundredth time, he looked back down into the whiteness. This time, there was movement! Surging beneath him was a vast stream of sheep being pushed ever further down the room by the strength of the wave created by their fellow animals behind. Excitement surged through him: soon he could act!

Eric's heart missed a beat as he saw the ocean of sheep stream towards his end. Soon the room was full, and as when Eric was a prisoner the sheep stood there, motionless, silent and identical. For one horrible moment, Eric feared the mix had failed. Then he remembered: that's exactly what he'd done until Nabi spoke.

Merly wasn't quite as keen on his creative role now. He didn't know what to do. Something had started to happen, that was certain. He'd been at the end of Nabi's corridor when he saw his friend's whole body tense and the rope prepared for action. The flaming torches on his coat burnt brighter than he'd ever seen before. Deciding to stay where he was until the drama unfolded, Merly sat down and waited, keeping a watchful eye on the distant Nabi.

All was still below, then Nabi's patience snapped like old elastic. With one mighty heave he tore the grating off, dropped the rope through and started his descent; the rope didn't reach the ground as he'd feared.

As he sped down the rope, he shouted to the sheep below, 'Get out of the way!'

To his delight, all the sheep looked up in amazement! When they saw an enormous fiery sheep hurtling towards them they needed no second invitation! They scattered like the sea splashing off rocks. Upon reaching the end of the rope he let go, readying himself for the impact ahead. His legs crumpled under him as the floor bought his fall to a dramatic stop. Over and over he rolled, knocking them over like nine pins until coming to a halt in a pile of bewildered sheep.

Quickly, he got to his feet, shouting, 'I'm Nabi, I'm here to save you, listen and do as you're told!'

A murmur ran through the sheep that moved out from Nabi like stone-driven ripples on a pond, slowly growing ever louder. The sheep closest to him stared curiously.

There were two very different reactions in the glass room. Strumphh's expression had gone from smug conceit through surprise to amazement, then horror, finishing up at nose-bursting rage.

White Mask and Toady knew they were finished and fled to the lift; they would have made it if Strumphh hadn't turned round and screamed at them.

'Come here!'

So great was the hold their evil master had upon them they couldn't break the tow of fear and stopped in their tracks.

'Sound the alarm!'

Toady pressed a large button on the wall and high-pitched alarms rang out all over the Facility. From everywhere, Nokemys started to converge on the huge room.

Eric knew that Nabi had done something, but what? He couldn't see! Then he heard whispers echoing quietly through the thin corridors. His heart leapt with joy: the mix had worked! Now it was his turn to act. He asked a reluctant

Cyril to fly back to the cave and tell Bardee now was the time. Anything to get out of here, thought Cyril, and using the last dregs of his courage, he was off like a rocket. Eric tore off the grating and jumped down.

If Strumphh was beside himself with rage before, it got a whole lot worse when he was confronted by a multicoloured sheep that seemed to appear from nowhere.

'So finally we meet,' he raged. 'Contemptible little animal. Do you really think you can beat me?'

They stood, looking at each other for a while, Strumphh's fury gaining momentum at every second. The staring match gave Toady and White Mask their chance. They were in the lift and gone, faster than Silveree could thought travel.

Eric was the first to speak. 'We come in peace; all we ask for is our own place to live.'

'You demand things of me!' he pointed at the sea of upturned heads below. 'You and your pathetic flock! I rule here!'

'You cannot beat us - we will have our freedom! Stay, work with us or go in peace.'

Strumphh, trying to control the fury that bubbled within, turned round and realised he was alone. There was nothing to be gained from staying, he raged: leave, regroup; his genius would see him through.

'Very well, I'll speak to my subordinates.'

'Thank you,' said Eric.

Strumphh waited for the lift and disappeared. The sheep was obviously an idiot. No one in their right mind would let an enemy of such brilliance go so easily. This would be simple!

He flounced out of the lift. Nokemys were running everywhere. Strumphh seized one and ordered the Facility sealed off. He would teach those renegades their final lesson.

Meanwhile, Merly had decided to act too. His fear of heights wouldn't let him climb down Nabi's rope, so bounding back through the corridors he looked for a grating over a lower ceiling. Finding one, he dropped through into an empty room. Taking his pipe gun out of his rucksack, he carefully opened the door. Before him was an empty corridor. He started to creep down it. Upon turning a corner he was confronted by the Chief Nokemy and two guards. It was difficult to see who was the more surprised.

The Nokemys went to draw their guns but Merly was too fast. He pointed his tiny pipe gun at them. There was a standoff for a few seconds before something popped into Merly's head; he had no idea where it came from but could not stop himself saying. 'I know what you're thinking. Does this tiny piece have one, two or three slugs up its pipe? The question you have to ask yourselves is: do you feel lucky? Well, do you?'

The Nokemys hadn't been feeling lucky for some time and certainly didn't feel any luckier now. Carefully, they dropped their guns to the floor. Merly's sigh of relief was almost audible.

'Now take me to the room with the sheep,' he ordered. 'And no tricks!'

Merly walked behind them with the gun at the Chief's back. No one stopped them, it was all too easy. When they finally arrived, they were stopped outside the door.

The Chief barked. 'Open the door!'

'No one's allowed in or out,' came the reply.

Merly dug the gun into the chief's ribs as a reminder.

'I have express orders from Generalissimo to negotiate with them! Open the door!'

The door was opened and banged shut behind them. Merly was staggered to see all the sheep turn towards him.

'Hi brothers!' he cried.

All the sheep that heard responded in kind. Merly's joy was uncontained!

One of the Nokemys turned to Merly. 'The gun, I've got to know.'

Merly pointed the gun in the air and pulled the trigger. Nothing happened! He nearly fainted with the shock! The Nokemy muttered something under his breath.

Nabi had heard Merly and navigated his way over to him. They embraced before Nabi saw the Chief.

Snarling fiercely. 'You have a sheep captive. Where is he?'

The chief didn't respond.

'I'll ask once more.'

The fearsome look on Nabi's face was all the convincing the Chief needed.

'Yes we have!'

Nabi took his pipe gun out of his rucksack.

'Nabi, they don't work!' warned Merly.

'Outside this room they don't know that and if I get one wrong word out of this creature...!'

The Chief had had enough and wasn't going to say or do anything.

Nabi growled to the Chief. 'Now get the door opened: ask one of them for his gun.'

The Chief banged on the door and shouted. Finally it was opened. He demanded a gun, which Nabi grabbed and pushed into the Chief's side.

The Nokemys went to grab Nabi but the terrified Chief stopped them. They edged their way down corridors until they reached a locked door that was hurriedly opened.

Before them was the most terrible sight Nabi had ever seen. Emaciated and lifeless, Arbe was stretched out on the floor. All the strange, back to front images on his coat had gone. His eyes were no longer blue and his coat was a dull off white. Nabi knew this was no time for sentiment; there was still work to be done.

'Pick him up,' he growled dangerously. 'Carefully.'

This they did and the sad little convoy made its way back to the huge room with the terrified Chief smoothing the way. Once inside, Arbe was laid carefully on the floor and Nabi let his emotions go. With Merly by his side he cradled Arbe in his arms, telling him how sorry he wasn't, that if he got well he'd never look after him and when they didn't get home he would always let him out of his sight.

Arbe opened his sad eyes and smiled at Nabi. 'Goodbye my worst enemy, I hope you never look after me and then everything won't be alright.'

The sheep closest by were sad and confused until Merly told them Arbe's world was back to front and if everything was all wrong, actually it was all right.

'How difficult!' said one of the sheep.

'You get used to it!' laughed Nabi.

'I need to stay awake now,' said Arbe.

In seconds he was fast asleep, snoring gently.

Merly looked at Nabi: he'd never seen him so happy.

Silveree had watched all this unfold and was pleased. He decided to go and tell the animals, who were desperate for news.

Cyril had never been so delighted to leave a building; fortunately, the last thing anyone was looking for was a butterfly. He flew like he'd never flown before; he even threatened the sound barrier. At the cave, Bardee was already in the Nepo. He didn't have time to finish telling them the news before the engines were started and off they went, an exhausted Cyril hitching a ride in Tien's wool. What a novelty to fly without using his beautiful wings! They sped quickly towards the Facility. Below them animals were streaming towards it, all hoping for good news.

As they approached the Facility, Bardee had a nasty shock. The concrete wasteland outside was already covered with animals. There was nowhere to land! Desperately, he looked around for somewhere but saw nothing. A dangerous thought struck him: could he land on the roof? Was it long enough? Could he stop? Tien could see the problem too and suggested they fly past and have a look. Bardee slowed the Nepo and flew over the roof, making aeronautical calculations as he went. There was no other choice, they'd have to try; it was going to be touch and go. Giving Tien the thumbs up, Bardee turned the Nepo towards the building and made his approach. The noise of the Nepo's engines terrified the Nokemys who fled into the building in disarray, causing more panic inside. White Mask and Toady were hiding. Inquisitiveness at the commotion got the better of them. They were awestruck by the Nepo as it thundered overhead. Not knowing what to do, hemmed in by animals with no sign of Generalissimo, they went to the huge room, demanding to be let in. By this time the terrified guards were past caring and opened the door. Knee deep in sheep, they stood quietly, trying to take in the events of the last few hours.

Bardee was glad he was flying into a stiff headwind. The smoke from the Facility chimney was spewing out parallel to the ground. This would help slow him down. He'd need all the experience he'd ever had and some he hadn't to pull this one off. Keeping the Nepo just above stall speed, he edged ever closer to the makeshift airstrip. Tien had an odd expression on his face and was gripping the edge of the cockpit tightly. Cyril wasn't enjoying it anymore; the only flying he was going to do in future would use his own power, not some ugly contraption that needed a runway. At least he could fly off the ghastly thing when Bardee had slowed down sufficiently, which is more than passenger and pilot could do.

The controls trembled and the Nepo juddered violently as Bardee used all his skill to reduce speed even more as the roof appeared a few feet below them. Bardee cut off the engines before pulling back hard on the stick.

The wheels barely kissed the ground. It was the best landing he'd ever done! Could he stop in time? Would the roof take the weight of the monstrous beast? Smoke billowed from the hysterically screaming tyres as Bardee slammed on the brakes. Sliding ever closer to the edge of the roof, Bardee fought desperately to stop the Nepo. Now he could see the upturned faces of anxious animals. He had to stop it! As a last resort he slewed the Nepo round, bringing it to a tyre howling, gut wrenching, nerve jangling, heart stopping halt. One wing was dangling over the end of the building and a wheel was no more than a foot from the abyss. Bardee slumped over the controls with relief. Tien sat there with the same odd expression; so hard was his grip on the cockpit edge he refused to let go, even though the ordeal was over. Cyril had become so mesmerised by the whole event he hadn't flown away. A look of terror refused to leave his face and he seemed to be staring at some spot in the far distance. They both came out of their trances at the same time. Tien prised himself off the cockpit edge whilst Cyril fainted. Bardee used his flying helmet to waft some cold air over poor Cyril, who opened his eyes, vowing to stay at home for the rest of his life doing nothing but look beautiful.

'Interesting. Most interesting,' gasped Tien. 'However, more excitement than is good for a sheep of my age.'

'Age has got nothing to do with it! I never want to go through that again,' said a relieved Bardee.

Bardee threw the ladder over the side and scrambled down before helping a wobblier than usual scientist, as the roof groaned ominously under the Nepo's weight.

Eric had thrown open one of the glass windows and was staring happily down at the throng below. Nabi saw him and rushed forward shouting. 'We've got Arbe!'

Eric's joy was complete. He was contemplating what to do next when the lift doors opened and there was a smiling, almost benevolent looking Walter Strumphh, accompanied by a Nokemy.

'I accept your terms, there is no reason we cannot live in peace and harmony. The time for strife is over!'

'Thank you,' replied a happy Eric.

'Are you all here, so we can make the announcement?'

'No, two of our band are missing.'

'Perhaps we should find them.'

Eric agreed and the Nokemy was dispatched on his mission.

A surprised Bardee and Tien were soon surrounded on the roof and taken to the huge room. Cyril, on seeing the Nokemys coming, had flown off as fast as he could before stopping not far away. Staring long and hard at his medal, agonising over what to do next, he came to the most momentous decision in his life: friendship was worth more than anything and he couldn't leave his friends to fend for themselves. After all, they might need him. Without a second thought he flew back, entering the huge room the same way as Nabi. Bardee and Tien were delighted to see their friends and the thousands of inquisitive sheep. Tien's heart sank, however, when he saw the grotesque creature with Eric in the glass room.

Eric waved to his friends, stepped forward to the edge of the room, then started his momentous speech. His coat of many colours shone so intensely it almost hurt his audience's eyes.

'I had a dream that one day all creatures would be equal and we would find our promised land. I had a dream that we would live in freedom and justice where no animal would be judged by size, variety or colour. Let freedom reign across all the valleys, plains, rivers and mountains. I dedicate this day to our brothers who have gone before. Their lives were not in vain. That we who inherit this freedom shall have a land ruled equally by the animals, for the animals, and freedom shall not perish from this land. Nokemys, take off your masks, feel the breath of liberty on your faces!'.

The Nokemys looked at each other uncertainly. Merly turned to the Chief and White Mask. 'Go on brothers, you can do it, now's your time.'

They hesitated for a second before tearing their masks off, jubilantly waving them in the air. Cheering echoed round the huge room as Nokemy after Nokemy followed suit. They were indeed kindly looking creatures. Toady was crying with the sheer relief of it all.

Then to Eric's amazement, a miracle started to unfold in front of him. The coats of the thousands of sheep below him were turning into colours of every hue; others had writing and signs appearing on their sides, faces and backs. It was the most wonderful sight he'd ever seen.

He wept with joy. A grill slamming down in front of him halted his trance like delirium. He turned to see Strumphh wearing a mask over his face. Strumphh knew he'd lost this battle but he vowed to win the war. Sanity had fled, all that that remained of his soul was putrefying evil.

'Words, words, cheap nasty words. Noble but useless. Did you really think you could trust me, you imbecilic cretin? Your freedom will be short lived. I shall dispatch you first, then the others.'

A look of dark insanity spread across his grotesque features as he gloated down at Eric and pulled a lever on the wall. A blue cloud started to fill the room. Eric clutched at his throat. Breathing was getting harder and harder. His short life had been in vain. Grief filled his soul. He seemed to be descending into darkness that grew blacker, blacker, blacker; then there was nothing.

In the huge room there was an eerie silence. No one knew what was happening but all feared the worst. Nabi had torn across the room and thrown himself against the shutter but he just bounced off. Tien and Bardee were frantically trying to open the door, with no success.

Strumphh waited for the cloud to clear before removing his mask and opening the shutter. Pulling a phial out of his pocket, he put it on the floor in front of him.

'See what happens if you defy me!' he shrieked. He picked up Eric's lifeless body and threw it to the sheep below. Nabi caught it, laying it gently on the floor. Eric's coat was now a dull white. Strumphh picked up the phial, grinning insanely down on them.

'When I drop this, all of you will die, all the animals outside, everyone. Only I and my kind shall remain to dominate this land. Enjoy your freedom while it lasts!'

There was silence as they all stared unblinkingly at him. As Strumphh was about to drop the terrible phial, Silveree appeared. Taking in the awful sequence of events in a nanosecond, he knew he had to act, whatever the personal sacrifice. Utterly distraught, knowing he was too late to save his dearest friend, he would make sure his death wasn't in vain. Time stood still as a triumphant Strumphh let go of the phial. There was a bolt of lightning as Silveree caught the phial and carried Strumphh away into the time space continuum. Silveree reappeared and collapsed onto the floor next to Eric. He had all but ceased to glow and was mumbling to himself in the strange language again. Nabi, Merly and Tien knelt next to him, knowing there was nothing they could do.

'We've done it, haven't we?' he gasped. 'Poor, dear Eric. It's my fault, I should never have left him alone.'

'Yes we've done it, thanks to you and Eric,' whispered Tien. 'You mustn't blame yourself.'

White Mask and Toady appeared. 'Is there anything we can do to help?'

They all looked at them, amazed.

'The fear's gone now.' said Toady, probably happier than anybody that his evil master had gone. For the first time in his life he didn't feel hungry.

Silveree gasped, 'Get them to open the doors, spread the word.'

White Mask did his bidding. Slowly, more and more Nokemys entered the room. Upon seeing their unmasked compatriots they too threw their helmets joyfully into the air.

They turned their attention to Eric. Tien knelt beside him and started to cry. Tears spread through the whole building. Merly and

Bardee were inconsolable; even Nabi shed a tear.

'What will we do without him?' cried Bardee.

'Look around you: see what Eric helped create!' said Tien. He was right: there were thousands of sheep eager to help in any way they could.

'We must take him back to the cave,' said Tien.

The saddest band imaginable solemnly carried Eric's body to the Nepo and gently laid him in the back. The animals filtered back into the forest, both happy and sad. Bardee couldn't take any more passengers due to the short runway so he vowed to come back for them. They all helped line the winged monster up on the roof. Bardee put the brakes on and revved the engines to full power. Brakes released, the surge of power pressed him back in his seat. Down the roof they sped until the end came in view. Bardee pulled back hard on the stick and closed his eyes, hoping for the best. The Nepo seemed as desperate as its pilot to fly. Falling towards the ground as it left the roof, it somehow managed to haul itself back into the sky. Upon landing, Bardee carefully carried Eric's body back to the cave and laid it on the normally upturned table. Tearfully, he covered it with their flag. Soon he was flying sadly back to his friends.

Tien addressed their newfound brothers and sisters, explaining all that had happened. Directing them as best he could to the cave, they were all invited to Eric's funeral. Then planning for all their futures would begin.

CHAPTER 15

THE END AND A BEGINNING

When all were safely back at the cave, arrangements for Eric's funeral were made. They decided on a solemn ceremony followed by an enormous party to celebrate Eric's achievements and the great new life ahead. Silveree had recovered somewhat but was still listless. He'd spoken of his sadness at never being able to travel by thought again and missed the other skills he'd lost. They tried to cheer him up. Slowly they were winning. His great joy was the friends he now had, although he missed Eric dreadfully.

Arbe, under the watchful eye of Nabi, was making a slow recovery. All the strange markings on his coat were beginning to reappear and his eyes were blue again. Everyone was being driven mad, trying to remember to say the right things, or rather the wrong things, in order to make him understand anything.

The evening of the funeral arrived, bringing with it a calm and clear evening. Animals of every kind covered the runway. Nokemys slowly filtered through the trees, taking their place at the back. Smaller animals were perched on the backs of larger ones in order to get a better view. Dusk fell as the guard of honour appeared, silencing the huge crowd. You could hear a pin drop. Sisu and Urho, representing the animals, led the way. Close behind came the sad band of brothers, carrying Eric's flag draped body, Cyril balanced reverentially on Merly's head. Never had he felt so sad; even vanity was forgotten. At the rear came Toady, White Mask and the Chief Nokemy. Eric's body was carried out to the runway and placed on a high rock so everyone could see the proceedings. The sad band of brothers took their places next to Arbe, who was not yet well enough to take part. Silveree was now able to hover, albeit feebly, and he took his place with the rest.

The night was calm, sad and peaceful. A warm light from candles lit the grieving group. Tien was the first to speak.

'I have lived a long and full life but never did I believe that I would be talking to you on this sad occasion as a free animal, unencumbered by fear. The books and writings in our home told me that a great leader would come and lead us to freedom. That leader was our dearly beloved Eric. In that great quest he succeeded but in so doing we have lost him forever. He gave his life for us. No greater sacrifice can an animal make than to lay down his life for others.'

He became unsteady on his feet. Bardee moved to comfort him. Tears welled in Tien's eyes as he tried to continue. Nabi and Merly stepped forward; together they steadied him.

Regaining composure, he was about to continue when a ripple of sound filtered through the huge crowd before him, slowly developing into a collective gasp of awe that refused to go away. Not knowing what to make of it, he turned round to his friends - then he saw it too. Stepping back in amazement, he pointed at Eric's body. The sad band turned to look. They too stepped back, filled with the same emotions as the rest.

Under their proud flag his body had started to glow, brighter and brighter. No one dared move; all were open mouthed and not a little fearful. The glow grew brighter still. Tien, fighting off apprehension, heart in mouth, approached Eric and pulled the flag off.

They couldn't believe their eyes! Eric's coat of many colours had returned and he was shining the brightest they'd ever seen, brighter even than when he gave his momentous speech. The little band huddled together and watched. Silveree didn't know what to make of it either; his expression was the same as the rest. There was a flash of blinding light that made them avert their eyes. The intensity of it lit up the entire runway. Upon turning back, they saw, hovering over Eric, shining brightly, another Silveree! Eric had stopped glowing and seemed more peaceful than ever.

The new Silveree wore a confused expression as it looked around. The old Silveree, however, did not. All his old strength seemed to return and he hovered and glowed with delight.

'Eric, dear Eric, welcome back!' He turned to the others, who to say the least were looking confused! 'Don't you see? This is where I'm from! This is how I came to be! Joy of joys!'

Even Tien's oversized cerebral cortex was having trouble grasping the implications of the last few minutes. The new Silveree's confusion seemed to be lessening. He looked at the lifeless sheep beneath him. 'I'm Eric, aren't I? Or at least, I was Eric.'

'You're still Eric! Only a new, different Eric,' cried Silveree joyously. 'This is truly a most splendid day!'

'Are you Eric?' stammered the baffled scientist.

'Of course I am, dearest Tien.'

He waved a short glowing arm at the little group behind.

'There's Bardee, Merly and Cyril! Arbe too! Rescued by brave Nabi I shouldn't wonder!'

Now they knew it was true, their grief turned to joy the like of which had never been seen. The news echoed back through the crowd, who cheered and stamped their feet, hooves and anything else they could hit the ground with. The noise became deafening.

Tien waved his arms, calling for quiet. Slowly, the noise drifted into silence.

'This day of sadness has become one of celebration! We have Eric back!'

Cheering started again. Tien waved for silence once more.

'First, we must bury Eric's mortal remains; then the party can begin!'

With great dignity and care, Eric's body was lowered into a grave. How strange and sad Eric felt, seeing himself disappear into the ground.

Silveree put a reassuring arm around him. A minute's silence was beautifully observed. Merly rushed to the high rock and shouted. 'Brothers and sisters, let the party begin!'

What a party it was! Silveree, taking strength from Eric, zoomed around above the party with him. Everyone danced, drank and ate until they could no more. Cyril gave intricate flying displays until so exhausted he retired to his bed for much needed beauty sleep. Nabi danced and danced and danced, amazing everyone with his dashing feet. Bardee strolled casually about, looking cool, as all fighter pilots do, taking the congratulations of everyone. Merly had met one of the many new lady sheep, and a beautiful one at that. Tien assured him her name was Nonomi Merraly, reminding Merly for the umpteenth time that the book was never wrong. Nonomi was a wonderful pink colour and had a pair of the brightest red lips down her sides that blew kisses as she danced. A romance seemed to be blossoming until he had one fermented fruit cocktail too many and fell asleep, much to his new lady friend's great displeasure.

Tien contentedly watched all from his position on high, full of wonder at the recent events. He was amazed at the riot of colour, shapes and symbols displayed on the coats of the thousands of happy sheep partying before him. Eventually, some fellow scientists joined him. Among them were Lali Geo, whose coat was covered with telescopes, and Tasi Nacewon who had a large bouncing apple on each side of his. They sat talking for hours. Tien was overjoyed as the full realisation of what they'd achieved sunk in. The party was slowing down when a jaded Merly came round. Not wanting it to end, he jumped back on the rock, shouting, 'Any brother musicians out there?'

Four sheep came bounding forward. Tien insisted on looking up their names in the book. There was Neboh Veet with piano keys down his sides, Vepeli Slerys with a microphone moving gently in his wool, Garti Norrs with a drum and drum sticks that appeared to be banging noisily against his coat, and Nopi Talcrec with a guitar that swayed back and forth as he moved. There was a frantic search of the cave for instruments. Eventually all was ready! The musicians ran on stage. Merly grabbed the microphone, shouting. 'Nabi, this one's for you: it's called Get Off, We Got Things To Do.'

The band struck up and Merly strutted about the stage, the notes on his sides appearing to bounce completely off him.

'We really need some leadership
Or we're all going down
He's laying there, a woolly mess
No signs of coming round
Go and see if he's breathing
Put a mirror to his nose
And if that doesn't seem to work
Tickle him on the toes

He's looking very weak
But I think he's trying to speak

Get off! We got things to do
What in the world are you waiting for?
We have no time to lose
Get off! We got things to do
We're in a world we're fighting for
And I'm not prepared to lose

Well I'll be dipped in treacle
That's a turn up for the books
You really can't tell a sheep's health
Just judging by their looks

Only half an hour ago
We thought he'd bought the farm
We panicked and we bricked ourselves
But it was just a false alarm

He's looking very weak
But I think he's trying to speak

Get off! We got things to do
What in the world are you waiting for?
We have no time to lose
Get off! We got things do
We're in a world we're fighting for
And I'm not prepared to lose.'

Eric and Silveree wandered in to the forest for some peace and quiet, hovering quietly together.

'Can I travel by the speed of thought?' asked Eric.

'My dear fellow, of course you can! Sadly my days of travel are over.'

'Can't you come with me?'

'My dear boy, why didn't I think of that?'

'Let's try.'

Silveree whizzed into the air before dropping down, bumping hard into Eric, joining their two glows together. Eric closed his eyes, thought for a second and they were gone! Seconds later, an amazed Tien saw a rather large Eric appear in front of him. There was a flash of light, followed by the sound of a balloon popping backwards, then Silveree shot into the air, reducing Eric to his normal size. Tien realised the implication immediately.

'This great day becomes more and more extraordinary!'

'Indeed it does!' cried Silveree. 'Free again to roam, and with my dearest friend!'

'What will we do without you?' asked a sad Tien.

'A brain such as yours will see it through, my clever friend!'

'I think I get most things wrong,' Tien said glumly.

'My dear fellow, simply not so. You got the genetic mix right. I didn't help you at all!'

'But what about the rest? All I do is blow myself up. Even I doubt their names are right.'

'What's in a name, my cerebral chum?' cried Silveree.

'You can do it. You are a great scientist and leader. None of this could have happened without you. My job here is done,' said Eric.

'I shall miss you, dear Eric, what adventures we've had!'

'Indeed we have! We'll be back from time to time. Wherever we are, we'll still see and hear you.'

Silveree and Eric put glowing arms around their dear old friend. Slowly, the number in the formula on Tien's coat started to change, finishing up:

$$E=mc^2$$

Eric and Silveree looked at it as it shone ever brighter and more golden. Now they knew everything would be all right.

'One question before you go. Where did you send that evil creature?'

'Somewhere he can do no harm, with lots of like minded friends: but it does get rather hot!' chortled Silveree.

They bade their final farewells before an oversized Eric hurtled into the air. Flying quickly over the crowd, he gave them a numerical firework display that lit up the sky for miles around. High above the runway's end he looked tearfully back, saw his friends way below and knew all was in good hands. He smiled at them before waving a fond goodbye. Below, the little band of brothers waved sadly back. Then he was gone.

Tien Sine, Merly Boab, Nabi Stolu, Bardee Thron, Arbe Sout and a fluttering Cyril watched his little comet trail disappear into the great beyond, before turning away to start their new life.